HALF-BLOOD

DRAGON

HALF-BLOOD
DRAGON

K.N. LEE

Cover designed by Danielle Fine
Edited by Cait Reynolds
Formatted by Ashley Michel

ISBN: 1542968313

DEDICATION

For My Family.

CHAPTER ONE

YOU'RE LUCKY TO BE ALIVE. Those words resonated in Rowen's mind as the noose was lowered over her head and secured around her throat, scratching her delicate flesh with its coarse banding.

Not so lucky now, she thought, noting that this was the third time she'd had this nightmare in a week.

Still, she couldn't awaken. Not until she had more information. If she was going to suffer in her sleep, she was going to at least figure out the cause of the prophecy, and the result. It was all she had.

Her only gift.

Rowen coughed as her airway began to close against the ropes. Was it supposed to be so tight? It didn't matter, the wooden floor would soon disappear from beneath her and she would either break her neck from the sudden fall or suffocate.

Neither option was appealing.

Rowen looked out to the crowd of blank faces. She ignited her second sight and dug deeper into the prophecy, summoning energy from the deepest depths of her soul. She could tell the difference between a dream and a prophetic scene. It was harder to awaken from a prophecy, and for good reason. There was something she needed to see to survive, if only for a few years longer.

The people that filled the square around the gallows were nondescript. No features to their faces, and no sounds from their mouths. No movement, either. They just stood like stoic silhouettes and stared at her as she awaited her death.

A black shadow stretched across the sky, blocking the sun and dimming the courtyard. While everyone looked to the sky, Rowen's gaze peered past them, to the gates.

But, wait. Something new was happening, something Rowen had never seen in the other dreams.

Someone stood at the far end of the yard, behind the crowd, cloaked in dark gray.

The mysterious figure lifted their hand and pointed a finger right at her.

Out of the silence that filled the crisp morning air, a whisper burned her ear.

"I'm coming for you."

Then, the trap door in the floor opened and the snap of her neck woke Rowen up.

A screech erupted from her lips as she woke up, clutching at her neck. Rowen shot up from her bed. A sheen of sweat glistened on her face as she struggled to catch her breath.

The nightmares. They were relentless. But, this time, a new element had been added to her prophecy. The fates were warning her, and she needed a plan just in case the time came when she needed to escape.

Something or someone was coming for her, and she wracked her brain for who that could be.

"They know," Rowen whispered into the darkness, as she struggled to catch her breath. Escape was the only way. Her plan to restore her mother's honor would have to be abandoned.

Rowen crossed the small room and gave the sleeping girl in the bed across from hers a gentle shove.

"Brea. Wake up. I need that favor you owe me."

A quick glance out the tiny window that looked out to the back of the palace showed that the path from the castle to the gates was clear.

"Really?" Brea yawned and sat up, her white bangs falling into dark almond-shaped eyes.

"Yes." Rowen lowered herself to her knees before Brea's bed. "Please tell me you will uphold your promise."

Brea tilted her head. "I promised to help you escape if necessary. I will do what I can, Rowen."

"But, what if we are caught?"

"No one will catch us. And, if they do, we are ladies-in-waiting for the princess. We can make something up. You're a clever girl. I'm sure you can talk us out of any situation. I've seen you do it."

"You are truly the best friend I've ever had," Rowen said, giving Brea's hand a squeeze.

"You as well, dear. I will miss you. We all will."

"I'm ready," Rowen said as she shoved on her traveling frock and boots. Once her cloak was secure around her shoulders and fastened at the neck, she strapped her money purse to her thigh. It would be unwise to leave with a bag. There could be no suspicion from the palace guards.

At first, becoming a lady-in-waiting for the princess seemed like a welcome escape from her stepfather's constant scrutiny. With her new life came hope and an opportunity to restore honor to her mother's family name.

Little did she know that Withraen Castle would be significantly worse. Since childhood her prophecies had been harmless. She'd always been one step ahead of whatever fate threw at her.

Now, a mysterious being haunted her. Remaining in the palace only led Rowen one step closer to the fate of her prophecy. She had to find a way to prevent that horrible death.

Ready, Rowen watched Brea dress herself. With a nod, they left the safety of their apartment adjacent to the princess' room and entered the dark hallway of Withrae Castle's east wing.

Macana, their chaperone, would be fast asleep in her room right beside theirs. If they were quiet, they could escape unnoticed. But, they had to be quick and confident.

Brea put a finger to her lips and nodded for Rowen to follow.

Rowen chose her accomplice wisely. Brea had a gift that could save them both if caught. They crept down the stone hallway, careful not to let the soles of their boots make any noise. Clutching her opal necklace, Rowen tried to keep her face free of fear as they walked past the princess' royal guards.

Brea gave one a nod, knowing that he was sweet on her.

The stairway at the end of the hall led to the back corridors and a series of secret tunnels that they'd practiced using with the princess in case enemies stormed the castle.

"This way," Brea whispered. She led Rowen down the stairs and to a large sitting room. She hurried across the carpeted floor to the paneled wall. Rowen chewed her bottom lip as she watched Brea feel around for the hidden door. With a push, it was opened, and freedom awaited on the other end of the tunnel.

"Come."

Rowen couldn't run fast enough. They slipped through the secret door and into the dark tunnel.

"Smells of old rainwater in here," Brea said, running her hand along the slick stone.

"I don't care, as long as we make it outside."

"Do not worry, dear. You forget what I can do."

Rowen hadn't forgotten. She was just hopeful that they wouldn't need Brea's unique ability.

The large stone door at the end of the tunnel was a beacon of hope. It was so close, yet so far. They couldn't help but quicken their speed to reach it. Reaching it was a small victory. Getting out of the castle's fortified structure would be a more difficult feat.

The dark cloak of night wrapped around Rowen and Brea as they carefully wedged the door open and slipped outside. The air was humid, and the sky a dull purple shade. Soon, the sun would rise, and dragons from all over would take to the skies.

To fly. Rowen closed her eyes and wished she could do what everyone in the kingdom did without effort. To transform and outstretch her wings would be bliss. But, Rowen could not fly. No matter how hard she tried.

Rowen rubbed her arm where a dull ache lingered from a failed attempt only years ago. It was her last attempt—one where she'd nearly killed herself trying.

Together, Rowen and Brea ran across the yard for what felt like miles. Breathless, they stopped just at the bars of the gate that reached high above them and ended at the stone structure that encircled the entire castle grounds. Four gates, and this was the one with the least amount of guards as it faced the cliffs that led right into the Perilean Sea.

"The guards are about to change shifts," Brea whispered. "I can carry you over the gate and land just beyond the main road. Then, we can walk to the Gatekeeper's station. She can port you home or wherever you want to go."

Rowen narrowed her eyes as she watched four guards leave their posts as four more walked toward the front post in their armor.

"Did you save enough coins for your trip with the Gatekeeper?"

Rowen nodded. "I saved everything."

"Good," Brea said, folding her arms across her chest. "You should be able to catch a port from Withrae to Harrow with four gold zullies."

Harrow, the biggest sea port in all of Draconia, and on the border that separated the human realm from the Dragon realm.

Her home.

The wind blew at Rowen, whipping strawberry blonde hair around her face as she wrapped her pale hands around the dark bars of the gates of the palace. The cold brass was soothing, despite the nerves that burned in her belly.

Freedom.

She yearned for it above all things in the world. For as long as she could remember, she lived her life for others, with no regard for her own wishes or desires. Back at the palace, there was a silent battle she had no clue how to fight. But, beyond those gates was an even bigger battle she was too afraid to face.

The world was vast. How long before she was swallowed up by it? How long before she ended up dead?

"Are you sure about this?"

"We can do it. The guards won't even see us if you hold my hand. See?" She peeled Rowen's left hand from around the bar and held it within her own.

A warm sensation filled Rowen's body as Brea held onto her. Rowen looked from Brea's dark brown eyes and down at her hand.

"Look, I can make you vanish as well. As long as we touch," Brea said with a smile as she used her vanishing gift.

Rowen's hand and arm disappeared before her eyes, and Brea was nowhere to be seen when she looked up again.

Clever gift. She wished she had a power as great as Brea's. Still, the ability to vanish could only get them so far.

There was another world out there beyond the dragon kingdom she'd grown up in. She'd read of vast oceans and mountains, human villages and fairies. Beyond the tall brass gates was a worn path that led to the center of the kingdom of Withrae.

Once they reached the city, what then?

The free clothes, room, board, and prestige were highly coveted. Rowen's mother would call her a fool if she showed up at home before her duties had been carried out.

Rowen chewed her bottom lip, her thick brows furrowing. This wasn't the time for doubts, but her options were limited. She needed more than a few coins to make it in their world.

"What's wrong?"

Rowen sighed and pressed her forehead to the gate. "I can't go back home just yet. The Duke would just send me back by first light."

The Duke of Harrow had always hated Rowen. She was a thorn in his side since the day he married her mother. For as long as she could remember, he sent her away for every training imaginable. Languages in Summae, dancing in Dubrick, embroidery at the School for Fine Arts in Luthwig. And at eighteen, he sent her away to be a lady-in-waiting for Princess Noemie of Withraen Castle. She was merely one out of seven ladies-in-waiting, yet she was singled out at every opportunity.

Brea put a hand on Rowen's. The red shimmer of her skin reflected the moonlight. In seconds, they vanished.

"Shhh, someone is coming," Brea whispered.

Rowen tensed and peered through the bars of the gate. A rolling cart pulled by a horse with a weary-looking old man approached the gate.

"Who is it?"

"I don't know," Rowen said. "I think he's making a delivery."

"Come," Brea said. "Let's just go back. If you're worried about Prince Rickard, don't. The prince will grow weary of pursuing you before you know it. Beautiful girls come to the castle by the boatload. His eye will wander."

"It's not just that," Rowen murmured. "I'm afraid."

"Of what?"

Rowen wrung her hands. "That something terrible is going to happen to me if I stay here."

Together, they left the gate and headed back to the castle. Brea took her hand and gave it a squeeze. "Then, we try another night. We make a plan. I'll transform and you can ride on my back."

"But, I'm just thinking of how lost I am. I have nowhere to go."

"Listen to me, Rowen. My parents aren't as bad as most Dragons. If you are a friend of mine, they would take you in with open arms. Not all Dragons are prejudiced toward half-blood humans."

"Most are," Rowen quipped.

Brea wouldn't know. She was a full-blooded Dragon from high society. She couldn't have known what Rowen had seen and experienced throughout her life. In Harrow, half-bloods were more common, and she'd witnessed the cruelty to her people. Her title saved her from most of the negativity, but it was always there in the eyes of Dragons.

"Go to my home in Kabrick. I'll send you with a letter. My father and mother can find you a new station."

"I don't want that, Brea. I don't want to be a burden. I want to be free."

"You want to go to the human kingdoms, don't you?" Brea asked.

With long white hair and a hint of red scales on certain areas of her olive-colored skin, Brea was considered plain by Dragon standards. Women of beauty had a brighter shimmer to their skin, and a glow to their hair.

Like Rowen's mother.

Rowen could never be as beautiful as her mother either. Short, thin, with dull gray eyes that never shown any light, and pale skin absent of any shimmering scales, Rowen was simply different.

Maybe that's why Prince Rickard chose to pursue her.

Brea smiled at her. "I don't blame you, Rowen. But, Draconia is your home."

"It's not as if I haven't thought of finding the human kingdoms. They are my people. It would be nice to be wanted and accepted for a change."

"You are half Dragon as much as half human."

Rowen stopped on the lush landscaped evergreen grass and looked to the pale moon above. "But, your race hasn't descended from humans in thousands of years. You hate them for betraying you. For hunting you down and trying to exterminate you."

Shrugging, Brea looked into Rowen's eyes. "I don't hate anyone. That's ancient history. Nothing to do with you and me."

"I know," Rowen said with a sigh, her eyes resting on the massive castle before them. She'd only been there a few weeks, but was already twisted in a web of lies and deceit, and a plan that would elevate her family.

But, only if she succeeded.

"Maybe one day I will go find the humans."

"You can't. You can't fly or fight, or do anything that would keep you safe."

Silent, Rowen chewed her bottom lip.

I can do more than you know. Sometimes she wished she could tell Brea her secret. Even though she was the best friend she ever had, she still could not trust her with the truth of her power.

"It's too dangerous to leave the safety of the kingdom. There are beasts and monsters out there. On land and in the sea."

"There are beasts and monsters inside as well."

They paused on the cobblestone path as a large black dragon flew overhead from the city and toward the palace. It lowered itself to the ground just before the main entrance, and shifted back into a tall young man dressed in fine clothes.

Rowen took a step back, hoping that he wouldn't look back and see them. Her face paled as he seemed to sense her presence and did exactly what she hoped he wouldn't.

Prince Lawson Thorne turned and looked right at them. In the torchlight, Rowen could only make out the hints of gold in his eyes. Her heart skipped a beat as their eyes met.

Rowen took Brea's hand into her own wishing they'd been invisible when the prince arrived. "He saw us." The thought of being caught and turned in by the prince struck fear into her heart. An excuse for being out after dark is what they needed, but her mind drew a blank.

To their surprise, he simply turned away, and walked up the stairs that led into his palace.

"Well," Brea said. "Aren't we lucky?"

Rowen swallowed with a nod, curious as to why the heir to the Withraen throne didn't seem to care that they were out after curfew. "Indeed, it's all I've ever been."

CHAPTER TWO

A DEATHLY QUIET SETTLED ON the tavern, almost as dead and quiet as the bloody remains of the man on the floor.

Elian Westin bent over and wiped his bloody fingers on the trousers of the dead man, curling his lip with distaste. He didn't mind death; he just didn't like the mess. The heavy stares and held breaths of the sailors, fishermen, and dock workers didn't bother him.

Treachery bothered him.

But, Cook had paid the price he had to have known was coming. After all, Elian was nothing if not clear in the exact degree of loyalty he expected from his crew.

Uncaring of the witnesses, Elian paused and centered himself, stilling his senses so that the tangible world wobbled, bending and revealing currents and waves of energy, emotions, and one soul about to escape a very dead body. He would not normally have taken in a soul like Cook's, after all, a man had to have some standards. But, the bastard knew too much, and to release a soul full of knowledge into the oceans of the Other Side would be foolhardy.

Pursing his lips, Elian forced the breath from his lungs. With a burst of unnatural power, he breathed in, frowning with the strain as he inhaled fiercely. Energy swirled, emotions snagged and tugged on each other, and the black shadow of a man's soul wavered, bending like a sapling in a storm toward the mighty pull of Elian's breath.

He called up more magic, his vision pulsing with the pounding of his heart. Cook's soul shook and fluttered in his direction, finally snapping away from the body like a topsail rope come loose in the wind. His lungs swelled painfully as he inhaled the soul through his lips. The soul burned as it went down, as if the man's last scream was silently clawing at the tender tissue of his throat.

Then, it was done. The world shivered back into solidity, with no one the wiser except for Siddhe, who gave him a look that was both shrewd and bored.

"The next one needs to be smart enough to keep his trap shut," he said to the woman.

She rolled her green eyes, being perhaps the only one who could do that to Captain Westin of the Wandering Star and live to do it again.

"This time, I want a Wordsmith, not just a scribbler."

Siddhe quirked her eyebrow. "Full abilities to transcribe memory?"

He nodded. She pursed her lips. He wasn't fooled.

She'd find him what he needed. She always did. That's why he kept her.

He began to smell the stink of the dead man soiling himself and decided he was done here. He glanced down one last time at the corpse on the floor then grinned at the barkeep. "Clean that up, will you?" he barked. "Bad for business, that."

The portly barkeep's frightened jump set his belly jiggling like a pudding, and it was with an amused smile on his face and whistle on his lips that Elian walked out.

The sun was beginning to set as he left the tavern. It never failed to strike a bittersweet chord with him that something as achingly beautiful as the sun turning the sky to flames and the ocean to glass could be inevitably and implacably accompanied by the putrid stench of the docks.

The wet rope and mildewed wood of a hundred ships clashed with barrels of fish heads and bait. Not to mention the simply lovely aroma of too many men and too little soap. This port of Lidenhold on the Agion Sea was just like all the others. Dirty. Smelly. Dangerous.

Elian shifted and settled himself underneath his tunic and jerkin. He'd be glad enough to get back to the ship tonight and soak in the deep copper tub in his quarters. It would be a good, quiet time to think, as well, and he needed to think. The loss of Cook was nothing, but his treachery could spell disaster for the hunt. He shrugged as if to shake the burden from his shoulders. It wasn't as if this hadn't happened before. He could deal with it. There was always a way.

He was so calm and certain, he almost convinced himself.

Siddhe came up and fell into step with him. He appreciated her silence. Once upon a time, he had appreciated her full breasts and the sway of her hips as well, in a vivid and detailed manner. But, every day closer to the Red Dragon was a day that his interest in such trivial things washed away like water grinding down a stone, though a man with his appetite could never bear to completely starve.

"Did Cook actually get a message out?" he asked.

"Yes, but I haven't found out to whom. Yet."

The 'yet' was telling. Siddhe was angry, though her expression was serene to the point of blankness. She didn't like not knowing, feeling like she had failed. She would chase this down until she got her answers, uncaring of the blood and chaos in her wake.

He liked that about her.

He also liked that her 'yet' had never failed him.

Yet.

The day it did? Well, with luck, that day would be a long time in coming. She was useful. He caught her twitching her mahogony braid over the swell of her breasts and felt a familiar stirring. Hopefully, a very long day in coming.

"It wasn't to any of the others," Siddhe said suddenly.

This stopped him in his tracks. He gave her his full attention.

"I can track anything that goes to the Spindlewald, the Black Fairy, or any of the other ships." She frowned. "Cook's message wasn't headed for any of them."

He waited.

"I don't think it was sent to a ship at all," she said finally and resumed walking.

Elian pondered her words, but not for long. They soon reached his destination in the miserable warren of dock houses and narrow streets. A wretched, battered little door to a sad, squat tenement of mud and sticks, liable to wash away as to blow over.

He knocked three times, and the door opened to reveal a plain girl, barely over the threshold into maidenhood. Stoop-shouldered and skeletal, she'd never be beautiful, and her life would be short. Her freckles reminded him of the spattering of stars he used for navigation in the night sky.

"Captain," the girl chirped, a wide grin revealing buck teeth.

"Cota," he answered gently as she ushered them both in. He didn't miss the way she wrinkled her nose at Siddhe or the way Siddhe curled her lip at the girl. He sighed inwardly. Women.

There were too many stale smells in the hovel, and Elian had no desire to try and pick apart their origins, each, no doubt, less savory than the last. A rough bench sat before a rusted brazier where a few forlorn coals wheezed out a pitiful amount of warmth. He and Siddhe took the bench while Cota bustled about the room, pulling chipped jars and pots from corners and piles of rags, assembling them before the brazier.

"Where've ya' been?" she asked cheerfully.

"Harrow."

"I ain't daft."

"Nor am I, young lady. And, is that any way to speak to your elders?"

She cackled, and Siddhe shifted beside him, resolutely looking anywhere but at the girl.

"How many before Harrow?" Cota asked slyly.

"Twenty-three." Twenty-three souls to feed his own.

"How many after Harrow?"

"Twelve." Thirteen, if he counted Cook's soul.

Cota snorted. "Not exactly making my job easy, now, are ya? Even fifteen would've been better for me. The more Dark Soul you've got on board, the easier I can swim through the visions."

Elian suppressed a smile at the girl's grousing. It didn't fool him at all. She was angling for more money. Just as she always did.

"It'll be like paddlin' through treacle today, it will," she grumbled.

"Double for today, Cota."

Like magic–he chuckled to himself–she was back to her usual spry movement and keen glances. Siddhe glowered, and he slipped his hand behind her to give her bottom a little caress and pinch. Her jaw twitched. All was well, then.

Cota began throwing pinches of powder and herbs on the brazier, poking the lethargic coals to life. Blue smoke began dancing up from them, pulsing, swaying, bucking. In Elian's mind, the forms became intimate, almost obscene in their motions. The hard walls of purpose and practicality melted, slithering away from his consciousness.

Ambition and desire bubbled up, drowning his thoughts. Then came indolence, indulgence, libertinage, gluttony, carrying him along on a tide that was rolling toward a shore of bright, blazing glory.

In a haze, he saw Cota kneeling motionless before the brazier. Her eyes were wide and unseeing, and her mouth hung open, a line of spittle hanging from her lips.

"Dragons in the water. Skies full of flames." Her voice was disturbingly sonorous. "Inside out. Upside down. The map will lead you to your heart's desire. Your heart's desire will be the death of you. Unless you learn to desire differently. Dragons in the sky. Oceans full of flames. Treachery for truth begets treacherous truth. That which you seek is not what you want. That which you want is not what you need. Lines are drawn by men. Both men and lines do lie. Water may tame a dragon, but a dragon can burn a ship. Pursue, but with caution."

Cota's head fell forward. Siddhe's snort rang in his ear. He blinked, the haze becoming nothing more than perfumed smoke, and Cota nothing more than a girl in rags.

"Well?" Siddhe demanded callously.

The girl shook her head and rubbed her eyes, but there was no cheeky smile that usually accompanied her predictions. She looked from Siddhe to him with dull, frightened eyes.

"Do we proceed?" Siddhe pressed.

"It's always a choice, ain't it?" Cota answered with a weak shrug.

"Tchah!"

Elian studied Cota, refusing Siddhe's quick pull on his sleeve to stand.

"Tell me," he said gently.

Cota slumped back on her heels and picked at the calluses on her hands. "It's conflicted, ya see? Used to be just one thing out there you were chasin', one thing you were wantin'. Now, there's two of 'em. But, I canna see if you're chasin' both or if one of 'em is chasin' you."

"Two?" Elian's head spun, and not from the residual effect of the drugs. There was only one Red Dragon. Nothing had ever mentioned a second one.

"Two," the girl affirmed, nodding wearily. "Near just the same."

For a horrifying moment, the room closed in on him. Two dragons. The Red Dragon and then... another? How could this be? It felt like a betrayal, yet he had no idea of who or what the traitor was.

Siddhe had clearly lost patience with the whole thing. She pulled him to his feet and gave the girl a scant nod before storming out the door. Numbly, Elian dug through his pocket and paid Cota double her price. He turned to leave, but was held back by a grimy little hand on his arm.

"I didna' like to say it in front of your trout-in-trousers," Cota whispered, a ghost of her old grin peeking through as she deftly insulted Siddhe's mermaid heritage. "But, there was one clear thing that came through."

He waited, hardly breathing.

"Withrae," she said. "Go to Withrae."

CHAPTER THREE

MORNING CAME TOO QUICKLY, USHERING Rowen out of the comfort and safety of her bed.

The night before had been sobering, reminding her that she was sent to the castle with a mission.

She was too close and too deep into the scheme to leave now.

Leesha, her personal maid from back home helped her dress for the day. She ran her hand along the silk which was nicer than anything she'd ever had at home, and every morning she loved the feel of it slipping over her skin.

But, not even that could erase the fear that left her hands shaking. She exhaled and closed her eyes. The mysterious newcomer to her dream wouldn't fade from her thoughts, even while awake.

"Ready for your jewelry, Mistress?"

Rowen nodded to Leesha.

Life in Withrae Castle was a show, and even Princess Noemie's ladies-in-waiting needed to be in costume.

She dressed in a long-sleeved gown over her undergarments and chemise. She slipped her feet into leather slippers and stood before her mirror. She looked tired. That much couldn't be denied. A long night of tossing and turning would make for a miserable morning.

"Where did Lady Brea go?" Rowen asked, noticing how Brea's bed was neatly made and empty.

"Macana summoned her earlier," Leesha said, keeping her brown eyes fixed on applying cream to Rowen's cheeks.

"Right," Rowen said. "I suppose I will see her at breakfast."

She walked over to their tiny window and looked out to the lake behind the castle. Memories of swimming in her own pond came to her. Days where she could do as she pleased were few and far between. But swimming had once been a favorite pastime. She and her younger sister would swim and pretend to be mermaids, saying that one day they'd both see and talk to a real one.

Sighing, Rowen turned away from the chill of the morning air. Mermaids. How ridiculous.

She wasn't any closer to her dreams but teetering on the verge of a bitter death. Her sister Ophelia was a full-blooded Dragon shifter and thus had been married off to a nobleman from a neighboring village at the age of fifteen. Rowen feared the opportunity to reunite might never present itself.

Not if her stepfather had anything to do with it.

"My lady," Leesha called as she fastened Rowen's opal necklace around her neck. "Are you feeling well?" She reached for a cloth. "Your nose is bleeding?"

Rowen took the cloth and turned away from the girl. She dabbed at her nose and handed it back. "I'm fine," she lied. She could never reveal the side-effects she sometimes suffered from using magic. Even if Leesha was her subordinate.

The castle was abuzz with activity and noise now that all the servants were awake and off to their posts. Rowen kept her head down as she navigated her way from her room to the dining room where the other ladies-in-waiting took their meals.

A quick breakfast was all she was afforded before she was expected to join the princess for whatever tasks and errands she may have. Withrae Castle would host a birthday feast for Prince Rickard the next evening, and the castle was in preparation for the elaborate festivities.

Relief washed over her as she saw that Brea had returned from her morning with Macana. Inside the small, elaborately furnished room was a sitting area for the girls and a dining table where they could eat when the princess dined with the royal family. The princess' portrait hung on the wall above the fireplace, in between two large windows that were opened to let in the breeze and sunlight.

Sausage awaited, with eggs, gravy, grapes and fresh bread. There was a tiered tray of sweet cakes and rolls in the center of the table, as well as wedges of orange jellies.

Her stomach grumbled as she lowered herself into the cushioned chair beside Brea at the circular table draped with an ivory cloth encrusted with golden embellishments. The warm fire at her back was soothing. It kept out the chill of the castle that seemed to seep into their bones no matter the season.

"Sleep well?" Macana, the chaperone to the ladies-in-waiting asked between sips of tea as a servant girl ladled potatoes onto her plate. Her indigo eyes stared at Rowen as if she knew her secret. "You look tired. Both of you."

Clearing her throat, Rowen glanced at Brea who looked away and took a bite of sausage.

Rowen noticed the bags under Brea's eyes and felt bad for waking her up for nothing the night before.

"Very well, ma'am," Rowen replied and busied herself with scooping thick gravy with her fried potatoes. "How did you sleep?"

"Don't lie to me, little miss. I know you two ladies were up chattering all night. Don't think I don't know what goes on around here. I see and know all. Do not forget it."

With a snicker, Brea looked up from her meal.

Rowen kept a blank look on her face. "No, ma'am. Never."

Macana lifted a crimson brow. Her white face was stiff as porcelain from creams crafted from the palace glamourist. One would never be able to tell that Macana was in her late fifties, when her skin was frozen to mimic that of a woman in her early thirties.

"I can't tell if you're a good liar or if you tell the truth. You're quite a challenge to read, Lady Rowen. In this business, that may work in your favor."

A small smile came to Rowen's lips. "Thank you, ma'am."

She did hate lying to Macana. It was her job to look out for all the ladies-in-waiting. She was kind to them all, and wise. Though she was like a mother, Rowen still didn't trust anyone.

Throughout the years, there was always a mother figure wherever Rowen was sent away to. But, none could ever compare to her own.

Macana shook her head. "Just as well. We have a busy day ahead of us. If you two chose to stay up all night, you'll be sorry for it."

Rowen ate heartily, yet left a bit of food on her plate as was customary for women of her rank.

"All right, ladies. You two are to join Princess Noemie for her dressing tomorrow. But, right now, I have an errand in the city," Macana said. "Rowen, you will join me."

Brea's eyes brightened. "Can I come as well?"

Macana cleared her throat. She seemed to mull over the idea before replying. "I suppose that would be fine."

"Brilliant," Brea exclaimed with a clap of her hands.

"What is the errand?" Rowen asked, just as excited as Brea, but her curiosity muted every other emotion she felt.

Tilting her head, Macana's dark eyes met hers. "Always the inquisitive one, aren't you?"

Rowen blushed and chewed the inside of her cheek. Macana never looked at her that way before. "Is it a secret, then?"

"That's it, Lady Rowen. It is a secret," Macana replied, standing from her seat to her full height which made her tower over nearly every woman in the palace. "We all have those, don't we?"

Rowen tensed at the way Macana looked at her when she said those last words.

Secrets.

Rowen didn't like those, especially when an unfulfilled prophecy loomed over her head.

She rubbed her neck as she and Brea left the dining room.

At least she still had hers.

For now.

CHAPTER FOUR

THE SCENT OF PERFUMES AND exotic spices filled Rowen's nostrils as she walked the streets of Central Withrae with Macana and Brea. It was almost like being free. She did miss the villages of her home, and the markets. They weren't nearly as loud and crowded as this, but had their charm.

The buildings that cluttered the city were tall and made of stone, with shops on the bottom and homes on the top. The wealthier stores had glass windows to display their goods, while others simply had a door with a sign hanging from above. Shopkeepers stood outside, ushering customers in, while young men and women stood in the streets, advertising their goods, or displaying them on hooks.

A massive Dragon guard stood in its dragon form on a platform behind the fountains, his golden eyes watching everyone in the square. His red scales were like armor, and his claws were longer than Rowen's legs. She stared at him, wondering what he looked like as a human. She imagined he was tall and muscle-bound, with big, heavy fists.

"You two stay close by. I just need to pick up a remedy from herbmistress," Macana said, keeping her thin hands firm on her change purse, as if someone was going to steal it right off her belt. If she was so afraid that someone was going to steal it, she should have hidden it inside her dress.

Some women liked to display their wealth despite their fear of having it stolen.

Rowen, on the other hand, kept her head down and tried to blend. She smirked and shook her head, scanning the Dragons that filled the stone streets, all dressed in their finery. The show of class was distinctive, with the lower-class ladies and gents covering their hair with caps or hats. Dragons of high class wore their hair long and proud, letting the shimmering strands catch the light like jewels.

The orange sky was overcast on that day, and there was little light coming from behind the thick clouds.

Rain. Rowen could smell it.

"We'll be right over there," Brea said, pointing to a cage of colorful birds near the center of the market. "With the birds and snakes."

"Very well. I will return shortly." Macana nodded and turned away from them to head into one of the double-stacked shops that lined the square.

"Look at these creatures," Brea said, pointing to the sleeping birds that perched on branches inside the cage. "I've never seen anything like them. They're so... fluffy."

"I have," Rowen said, coming for a closer look. "They are snow owls. I've seen them in scrolls during my studies of the other kingdoms and lands. They sleep during the day and hunt at night. They're from the human realms."

"What a fascinating name for such a beautiful creature." Brea gave her a look. "That's why you're such an awful dancer. You spent too much time studying books that will never benefit you at court."

"Who says? My studies have suited me well. Dancing is a silly practice. I'd rather woo my future husband with my wit, not how well my feet glide across the floor."

Brea chuckled. "Nonetheless, we should buy one of these owls. We can get it a pretty cage and bring it to our room. It can watch over us while we sleep."

"That doesn't sound frightening at all," Rowen said under her breath as she wrapped her hand around the cage bars.

An owl opened one brown eye and looked right at her. The eyes weren't like those of other birds. They reminded her of those of humans. Intelligent. Perceptive.

She held her breath. It was as if the creature read what was in her soul and wanted her to understand that it knew ever secret she'd ever kept. She shivered and let go of the bars.

"What is it? Did it bite you?"

Shaking her head, Rowen watched the owl, waiting for it to speak. Instead, it closed its eye and went back to sleep.

"No. It just looked at me. It was odd."

"You're odd, Lady Rowen."

"I've heard."

"What do you say? It'll look adorable on our wardrobe."

She cleared her throat and looked to Brea. "Then, you can have two oddities for your human realm collection."

"Human realm collection?" Brea shoved her with a laugh. "Come now. Don't joke about such things. You're my friend. This will be our pet."

"I'm not keen on keeping pets, Brea," Rowen said, looking away from the owls and back toward the shops. "Every creature should be free."

Without another word, she headed across the square toward the herbmistresses shop. Ivy and flowers covered her door and glass storefront cased in stone. Herbs were the closest thing to magic the Dragons of Draconia had other than whatever abilities they were born with. It was astounding what the perfect concoction could do in the hands of a capable master.

"Where are you going? I said we'd be at the bird cage."

"You did. I said no such thing."

Rowen wondered what surprise Lawson had for her. She could not wait to be done with the dreaded birthday celebration to return to him. Perhaps tonight they could share a bed. It would draw them closer, but would also put her at risk. She needed to maintain her innocence until after marriage. Then, her body would be his and she would love him for an eternity.

It was the perfect reward after eighteen years of suffering.

Still, she wondered what life as a queen would be like. Would the people of Draconia ever accept her? Rowen's mother had given up everything to keep and raise her. She could have sent Rowen away and returned to her life as a respected Draconian noblewoman and upheld her betrothal to the king of Frostwert.

Rowen was grateful for her mother's love. Before Lawson's, it was all she'd ever known.

She pushed open the door to the herbmistress' shop and was greeted by the overwhelming smell of jasmine, and what she recognized as burnt hair.

Cringing at the odd combination, Rowen covered her nose with her sleeve and stepped inside, letting the door swing closed behind her. It was quiet inside, and empty. She looked at the many rows of shelves stacked with bowls and jars. The sound of whispering came to her as she approached a table of bundled herbs arranged neatly in a flat wooden box with several exposed compartments.

Rowen recognized Macana's voice and stepped closer to the closed door at the back of the shop. She suspected that Macana was up to something. Only those that had things to hide were worried about what others were hiding, and at breakfast, Macana was especially keen to know what Rowen hid behind her innocent looks.

She pressed her cheek to the cool wood and closed her eyes.

"You think I'm a novice?" a squeaky voice asked on the other side of the door. "It will work. Now, get out of my shop before I pop you with my cane.

Rowen gasped as the door opened and she was met with Macana's surprised expression. Surprise was quickly replaced by disapproval.

"Nosy girl. I told you to stay put."

"Actually, you just told us to stay close by," Rowen replied.

Macana's cheeks reddened and her nostrils flared.

"Insubordinate little wench," Macana said. "I am your superior in every way. Do I need to remind you of that?"

The small herbmistress used her cane to tap Macana on the behind. "Move, woman. I have work to do."

Rowen stepped aside so that Macana could leave the doorway. She watched the herbmistress return to her work station. Her eyes widened when she noticed her black, wiry wings flapping behind her small frame. She was older than the both of them, with short gray hair and big purple eyes. Her eyes were pointed at the top and were pierced with shining red stones.

A fairy.

At barely three-feet tall, the fairy woman lifted herself into the air and grabbed a satchel of herbs from the highest shelf. She threw the glittering dust into a pot and used her cane to stir.

"I asked you to leave," she said, glaring at both Macana and Rowen.

Macana grabbed Rowen by the wrist and pulled her from the shop.

Once outside, Macana clutched Rowen by her cheeks and lowered her head to a few inches from her face.

"One day, your snooping will be the end of you. You hear me?"

Rowen's brows furrowed. Macana's fingers dug into her cheeks, making them burn. She sucked in a breath as Macana lifted her from the ground and held her in the air.

Macana's strength was surprising, and Rowen knew better than to retaliate. When Macana shook her, she chewed her bottom lip and fought to restrain herself.

"You hear me?" Macana asked, clenching her jaw.

"I do. Sorry, Lady Superior."

Macana didn't let her go right away. Instead, she glared at Rowen as if to drive home the fact that this would not be the last of their discussion.

"I know girls like you. I've seen them come and go throughout my years of service to Withrae Castle. You think because you are young and beautiful that rules do not apply to you. Well, young lady, they do. More than ever. You watch yourself and mind your business if you want to survive."

"Yes, Lady Superior."

Macana grimaced and dropped Rowen to the ground. "And, don't forget that I may be older, but I am more Dragon than you will ever be."

Once released, Rowen stretched her cheeks and frowned as Macana turned and walked away from her. Whatever that was about was probably more serious than the secret Rowen kept. And, she feared that she may have heard more than she should have.

"Dear spirts," Rowen said in a breathy whisper. "Save me."

As if to deny her prayer, lightning crashed and rain poured onto her face.

"Subtle," she murmured, frowning at the gray sky as she shielded her eyes with her hands.

CHAPTER FIVE

THE NEXT DAY Rowen and Brea visited the princess' elaborate private apartment that stretched nearly the length of the back end of the palace.

Rowen stepped inside with a sigh. After her encounter with Macana the day before and the nightmares that haunted her every time she closed her eyes, she was ready for a distraction of any sort.

Princess Noemie had no shortage of work for Rowen. So, she was confident that the day's activities would help clear her mind.

Princess Noemie stood with her back to them as they entered her private quarters. Her long black hair was already styled, tied tight into a bun on the top of her head and encircled with tiny jewels and a diamond encrusted comb.

Seamstresses and the master clothier all worked to fit her for her gown for the evening while Brea and Rowen waited to be summoned forth.

"Ladies," the princess said, glancing over her naked shoulder. "Why don't you pick out a satin sash for your dresses,

We should all look remarkable this evening. I can't have you standing next to me in anything less than the best."

Brea's eyes lit up and she grinned. "Yes, your highness."

Rowen followed her lead and walked over to a table covered in rolls of beautiful fabric. There were ribbons and jeweled combs for their hair.

"I'll be wearing gold," Princess Noemie said. "So, pick anything but that."

Lady Ishma leaned in close to Rowen, her warm breath on Rowen's ear. "Or red," she said.

"Why not?"

Lady Ishma snickered, looking from Rowen to Lady Ambeth, another lady-in-waiting with golden hair and thin blue eyes. "They say it's Prince Rickard's favorite color."

Rowen cheeks flushed. "So, everyone knows?"

Lady Ishma's smile vanished and she took Rowen by the hands. "Knows what, exactly?"

Rowen pulled her hands away and rolled her eyes.

"Oh," Lady Ishma said, feigning a revelation. "That Prince Rickard covets your pure body? Of course, dear girl. You think we don't notice the way he looks at you? And dear, when he nearly slapped you at the first half-moon ceremony after your arrival... we all knew it was because you denied him. The prince has a hearty attitude, and an even heartier vigor for new women. It isn't wise to anger a Dragon such as him. Best to sate him and be grateful he even cast a gaze your way."

Brea frowned. "Have you no heart? Maybe she truly doesn't want Prince Rickard's attention."

Ishma shrugged, her brown curls rolling off her shoulders. "Who needs a heart when you have my looks? We all know that whatever front you put up for the prince is futile. So, why doesn't she just get it over with?" She ran her fingertip across Rowen's bosom, her smile widening. "A Dragon mates for life... with other Dragons. What would he want out of a human other than a night of curiosity?"

Now, Rowen's cheeks burned. The other girls were perceptive creatures. What they believed they saw was false, but, how long before they learned her real secret?

"I am sure you're right, Ishma. Then, he can be all yours. Correct?"

Ishma nudged Rowen in the shoulder. "Precisely. You are a quick learner. There is hope for you yet. I hate to remind you, but I am a full-blooded Dragon."

Ishma was ranked higher than Rowen, and slept in the princess' room. It was best not to anger the young woman. Her influence with the princess was much greater than Rowen could ever dream.

Rowen snatched a green sash from the table and turned away from Ishma and the other ladies. She left them to sit on a stool near the princess. It was as far away as she could go at the time. Until she was relieved of her duty, she would bathe in the safety of Princess Noemie where the girls would keep their mouths shut about her brother.

She fidgeted with her necklace, bottling her anger inside. She wished that she could return to her room and take a much-needed nap. Then again, the nightmare might return.

When Princess Noemie's blue-eyed gaze landed on hers, Rowen smiled at her. They were all fortunate to have a fairly just master, even though she had the power to ruin them all from the slightest offense. It was a dangerous dance they all did, to keep the princess happy, when her moods were as flighty as a raven.

"Lady Rowen," the princess called in her sweet soft voice, breaking Rowen from her thoughts. She was tall, but thin, with blue scales that littered her skin in beautiful patterns, and hair that emitted a faint blue glow in light or dark.

For Dragons to look down on Rowen for being half-human, they certainly coveted those with less visible scales and more pure skin. Princess Noemie was fortunate to only have scales on her wrists and the back of her neck.

Rowen bowed her head. "Yes, your highness?"

"Can you deliver a note for me? I'm afraid I'll be too busy with the day's activities to deliver the message myself. Besides, you've always been so discreet for me."

Rowen stood. "Of course. Whatever you need."

"Thank you," the princess said. She nodded toward the small table before her, and a white note placed before a vase of chrysanthemums. "It's right there. Grab it for me."

Rowen did as she was told. It would be nice to leave the presence of the other girls for a bit. The princess was notorious for sending letters to ladies of the court, inviting them to secret parties and games in her private apartment.

"Who shall I deliver it to?"

The princess yawned as the master clothier tied the gold sash around her tiny waist.

"Take it to my brother."

"Which one?" Rowen hesitated to ask.

"Prince Rickard. And, be quick about it. I have several more errands for you before the feast begins."

CHAPTER SIX

ROWEN DREADED HER VISIT TO
Prince Rickard's private apartment. She was
anxious to make it through the day without
incident.

Ishma's words nagged at her. Rickard was just playing with
her, and that was fine. Her sights were set a bit higher than the
young prince.

The two uniformed guards outside his door barely paid her
any mind, having knowledge that she was a lady in waiting for
the princess.

She knocked on the door and swallowed, waiting.

The wait felt like an eternity, and she almost slipped the
note under his door instead, and ran off in the other direction.
To be in such a position was not new to a lady-in-waiting. It was
customary for the royal Dragon males to take mistresses from
ladies of noble birth before they settled with their eternal mate.
It did benefit the woman, elevating her station and at times
made her a more desirable potential wife to the men of court
or other noblemen.

Despite that, Prince Rickard wasn't the kind of man Rowen saw herself losing her innocence to. He was more than a prince. He was a pawn in her game.

A dangerous one.

She inhaled as the door cracked open.

The moment Prince Rickard saw her face from the crack in the door, he flung the door open and backed away from her, yawning.

"What do you want?"

Rowen hesitated to step inside. She caught a glimpse of the foot of his bed in the bedroom portion of his private apartment. A woman's slender legs were visible as she stirred under the blankets.

"You weren't in your room last night."

The fact that he just revealed that he'd come looking for her in her room turned her blood cold.

Rickard noticed her surprise and grinned, stalking over to her with the arrogance he was known for, his bare chest exposed and his pants low around his narrow waist. The fact that he had another woman in his bed didn't stop him from cupping her face with his hand.

A rush of warmth filled her and her eyes fluttered closed. The touch of a Dragon was euphoric and left her a bit woozy on her feet.

"Where were you?" Rickard asked in a whisper that sounded more like a purr as he lowered his face to her neck. He smelled her and groaned. "With a page? Or a palace guard? Go on. You can tell me."

"I did not know to expect you, Prince Rickard," Rowen said and chewed her bottom lip, torn between hoping he would remove his hand and desperate for him to never let go. "I just went for a walk."

Prince Rickard removed his hand from her cheek and tilted her head up so that their gazes met. Dark like the sea at night, there was nothing in his eyes but pride and arrogance. She regretted not taking her chance to escape, but knew what she must do to survive. His full lips curled into a smile as he examined her face.

"I think you know more than you let on. That little face of yours hides the truth better than anyone I know," he said. "You're lucky I fancy you, or I'd tell Macana that you weren't in your room last night. Perhaps I should tell her anyway. To show you your place."

And, she'd know that you were pursuing me. Rowen kept her mouth shut.

"She'd have you whipped until your rear turned red as a rose."

Rowen's brows rose. "Is that what you wish? To see me thrown out of the palace and cast back to my family in shame?" She covered his hand with her own. "I thought my place was with you, your highness. Now that you have me, what will you do with me? Shall I undress now? I think we have time before you're called to council with your father and brother. If you're quick."

Rowen flickered a glance to his bed. "Shall I just lay beside the woman you already have in your bed?"

As expected, Rowen's sudden change of attitude baffled the prince. He took a step back and beheld her with an odd look as if he finally saw her as more than prey. Then, he laughed heartily.

His scales were as black and stood out on his naked bronze skin, faint. They caught the light spilling in from the window that stretched from the floor to the ceiling. Freshly out of his teens, Rickard was handsome. He was bearded, unlike his older clean-shaven brother, and usually wore his hair tied at the nape.

"I swear I think your mission is to vex me," Prince Rickard said, raking a hand through his dark, shoulder-length brown hair. "The beautiful human walks into my castle and continues to ignore my shows of affection. What game are you playing?"

Ignoring his question, Rowen straightened her dress and pulled the letter from her sleeve. "I've come to deliver this letter from Princess Noemie."

Rickard nodded and snatched the letter from her grasp. He tapped the letter onto the palm of his hand and watched her. "I will figure you out, little human. Mark my words."

Rowen narrowed her eyes as she examined Rickard's face. He was an interesting specimen. If there was one thing she wished her mother had taught her, it was about men.

"I am sure you will, your highness."

"You're lucky I have to leave soon. I'd ravish you right here on the floor."

Rowen rolled her eyes. "I am sure you would."

Startling her, the prince caught her by the wrist. His grip was too tight, and pinched her skin. Whatever euphoria she felt after his earlier touch was replaced with fear.

He brought his face close to hers. "Do you mock me, human? I have a mind to find out what you were really doing last night."

"Forgive me, your highness," Rowen said quickly. The last thing she needed was to have Prince Rickard following her and getting into her affairs.

Rickard's growl made the hairs on the back of her neck stand on end.

"Silly little fool," he breathed, pushing her against the wall. "I think I like you even more with each passing day."

That feeling of desire and pleasure returned at full force and Rowen sucked in a breath.

Her skin grew tight and warm as his fingers ran along her clavicle.

A guard stood in the doorway, abruptly ending the moment.

"Your highness, my apologies. You've been summoned by the king. Urgent business."

Rowen slipped from her place before Rickard and past the guard.

Once outside, she exhaled and fanned her cheeks. For hating him so much, he knew how to leave her flustered every time they were faced with one another.

CHAPTER SEVEN

AFTER LUNCH, MACANA STOPPED ROWEN in the hallway once the other ladies left to finish helping the princess with her preparations.

Warnings flashed inside Rowen's head at Macana's touch. She flinched and took a step back as if her hand had touched a flame.

"What is it?" Rowen asked as sweetly as she could without sounding suspicious.

Macana's eyes narrowed as she looked Rowen over. "I have an errand for you."

Rowen nodded. "Of course," she said. "What is it?"

After looking over her shoulder toward Princess Nome's sitting room, she pulled a letter from her bosom.

Frowning at the letter and where it had been, Rowen silently accepted. It would take weeks to regain Macana's trust, but Rowen knew that deep down her opinion of the Dragon before her would never change. She kept her mouth shut, but thought of just what she'd do if Macana assaulted her again.

She'd show her just how much Dragon's blood she had running through her veins.

"Take this to the gentlemen's sitting room. Give it to Lord Mulligan."

Nodding, Rowen turned to execute her wishes.

"Have you nothing to say?" Macana asked.

Rowen grimaced. As she turned to face Macana, she put a smile on her face. "Why?" Rowen asked. "Is there something you'd like to say?"

"Not particularly," Macana said, her face absent of emotion. "Run along."

Rowen left Macana with a sinking feeling in the pit of her stomach.

She hurried along the long halls, away from Princess Noemie's dressing to one of the sitting rooms where noblemen spent their days playing cards, telling awful jokes, and drinking the finest wine the castle had to offer. The king of Withrae treated nobility well, and they spent more time in the castle than they did at their own estates.

Whatever business Macana had with one of the lords was not of her concern. She just wanted to be rid of the letter and to return to the princess. Somehow she felt safer there, with royalty to protect her.

Rowen yelped when she passed by an open door and was yanked inside. Strong arms pulled her and wrapped around her frame.

To her surprise, she looked up into the eyes of Prince Lawson, the heir to the Withrae throne.

"There she is," he said, and lifted her into the air. Her skirts flared as he spun her around the room.

"You nearly sent me into shock, Prince Lawson," Rowen said with a breath of relief. Her fear was replaced with a genuine smile. "But, I will forgive you this time."

He grinned and kissed her on the lips. "You'd better," he said, and set her down on her feet.

"This is a surprise." Rowen looked around Lawson's private study. There were two rooms, one with his desk, shelves of collectibles and scrolls, and another with sofas and a fire place. "What has you so enthused this fine morning? It's not your birthday."

She spotted a small round table set with food and wine. A drink sounded like a good idea.

"I have some good news," Lawson said, sliding his arms around her small waist. She loved the feel of her body against the hardness of his. This was one thing she would miss if she ever did need to make a quick escape.

That gave her an idea.

Pouring herself a glass, Rowen grinned. This was a pleasant diversion from her endless tasks of the day. "And, what is that?"

She took a sip of wine. The sound of a book closing caught her attention.

Rowen's smile was wiped from her face when she saw Prince Rickard in the sitting room with his legs propped on the side of the seat.

"Lady Rowen?" Prince Rickard asked, his eyes widening as he looked her up and down. "This is the lady you're planning on ruining the sanctity of our blood line for?"

"Yes," Rowen said, answering for Prince Lawson. This time, she truly faked her confidence. Her idea was to ask him for protection. Now, she was afraid that Prince Rickard's knowledge of their affair would threaten everything she'd built.

Her voice wavered and her eyes watered as she fixed her gaze on the prince who sat on a red sofa. He had a booklet in his hand, one with a strange symbol on the cover.

Rickard looked from Rowen to Lawson. "You sneaky bastard."

"Listen," Lawson said, holding his hands out before him, as if to keep Rickard from lunging from his seat at Rowen. "Nothing has changed. I confided in you about the woman I loved, and you told me you supported my decision. Well. I chose Rowen, over all the women in the kingdom."

For a moment, the silence was agonizing. Rowen's heart wouldn't slow no matter how hard she tried to calm herself.

"You're serious?" Rickard asked, lifting his brows. "Like, utterly serious?"

Lawson's jaw tightened. "I am."

"Well," Rickard said, surprising them both. "I'm starving." He stood and walked toward the main exit back into the palace.

Lawson laughed, a bit nervously. "What?"

Rowen remained tense, and waited to exhale.

"I'm starving. I'm going to find some food. Do what you want with your life."

"I will," Lawson said, with finality.

Rickard took Rowen's glass of wine from her grasp. The look he gave her when their eyes met and he drank down her wine turned her blood cold.

Instinctively, Rowen stepped away and folded her arms before her as Rickard held her gaze. She could feel cheeks paling as she read the truth in his eyes. The silence was agonizing. But, she could read what he hid behind his cool attitude.

He now hated her.

And this would not be the end of this.

As if he knew that she recognized what he was thinking, Rickard cracked a grin. "She's a bit of a bore, Lawson. But, so are you."

Lawson sighed and they both watched Rickard leave the study.

Once Rickard was gone, Lawson turned to Rowen.

"That wasn't so bad, was it?"

Rowen fell to her knees, overcome with nausea.

"No, Lawson. It's worse than you know."

CHAPTER EIGHT

"**H**OW COULD YOU TELL YOUR brother? He is the last person I wanted to know," Rowen said, her palms wet with sweat. She rubbed them against her dress and closed her eyes. "He will ruin everything."

"What was I supposed to do, Rowen? I turned to the one person I trust for advice. He's my brother and that fact will never change."

Rowen's eyes narrowed as she looked up at Prince Lawson. "Advice about what?"

"About you!"

To her surprise, Lawson's usual smile was absent from his face. She didn't like the way he looked at her, as if she'd stolen something and he'd caught her.

"What do you mean?"

"You forget that I saw you outside of the castle just last night."

Groaning, Rowen pushed herself up to her feet. She straightened her dress and returned to the table of wine and cheese. Picking up the glass Rickard had taken from her grasp, she poured herself another and drank it down.

Just when she thought the day was going well. It wasn't a surprise. For Rowen, whenever things did go her way, something terrible always followed. Perhaps this was the worst of it. She licked her lips and stared at the plate of assorted cheese. She could figure this out.

Rickard was just an impulsive young Dragon. Maybe this would work in her favor. Perhaps this revelation would cause him to no longer pursue her. She rubbed her temples.

No, that wasn't like Rickard at all.

"What were you doing last night?"

Sighing, Rowen looked to him and shrugged. How could she tell him the truth? Her love for him was strong, but her survival instinct was stronger.

Her love for Lawson made her weak. She didn't know how to hide her emotions from him the way she could from others.

"I was afraid," she admitted.

Lawson took her by the hand, sat down in his arm chair and pulled her into his lap. "Of what?"

Instead of meeting his gaze, she kept her eyes down. She couldn't hide the truth from him forever.

"Rowen," he said, and tilted her chin. "Look at me. Tell me what troubles you. If there is one person in the kingdom that can fix it. It is me."

Rowen looked up and their eyes met. Sometimes she wondered if she was part of his game, and just thought she was the master of it all. His bright green gaze nearly took her breath away no matter how many times she gazed into them.

The flecks of gold around his iris were unlike anything she'd ever seen. She touched his hair, trying to formulate her words.

Lawson's black hair was styled in the fashion different from the upper-class, long and tied into a knot on the top of his head. It was different, but fitting. Rowen was certain that after the party, everyone would be wearing their hair just like the future king.

It wasn't hard to fall for Lawson. She was lucky in that respect.

"I just worry. You can have any woman in the seven Dragon kingdoms. But, you chose me. That's frightening. Do you know how many people hate me already? Just for who and what I am. We both know that your father will never let you marry me."

"Listen. We will find a way to make this work. But, seeing you out last night worried me. I thought you were trying to slip away in the dark of night. I thought I'd lose you."

"No. I wasn't trying to leave you. I just worried that things may never come to fruition. I don't like secrets. Your brother doesn't hide his feelings. Why do you? He can go around the kingdom collecting mistresses like prizes, and fighting in the streets like a madman."

She kept her face free of the joy she felt for her expert manipulation. Prince Lawson would have never noticed her if his brother hadn't hit her in front of everyone at court. It was her way into his heart. Through his compassion. Now, all her work was in jeopardy. How long before Rickard told others?

He stroked her back and sighed. "My brother is reckless. He will never make a good king. But, he has a good and loyal heart, and when he does find his true mate, he will do as every

Dragon does and will be devoted to her for life. The same as how I intend to be devoted to you."

"But, I am not a full-blood. You might change your mind."

"Nonsense," Lawson said with a smile that wasn't as convincing as she'd hoped. "I could never leave someone as beautiful as you."

Rowen sighed. Her beauty could only take her so far. She covered her mouth with her hands and exhaled.

"I just don't like Rickard knowing. Something about it doesn't feel right."

"Can you fault me for telling him first? I assure you, I will tell my father soon, and we will make this work."

"I suppose," Rowen mumbled.

"You see, I'd prefer to keep my plans quiet, so that no one can ruin them. When the time is right, I will make it known to everyone in the kingdom. Lady Rowen Glenick has my heart, and will one day be my queen."

"Queen of Withrae, Harrow, and all the cities of Draconia. My stepfather would just die from the shock of it." She shook her head. It didn't seem possible.

"That's right. You just sit tight and let me worry about the laws and tradition."

Nodding, Rowen rested her head on his shoulder. She breathed in the scent of the cream his valet used to shave him, and felt as though she could stay there, wrapped in his arms, forever.

"I remember when you first came to the castle. While there were whispers of the only known half-blood being in our castle, I was intrigued by you. Not because you are half-human, but because there was something special not everyone could see.

I'm happy that you are the first human to live and work in my castle. No other Dragon kingdom can boast of such a thing."

"Some might say otherwise. Some might find it distasteful to have the bloodline muddled by human blood. And, some might be offended to have me on the throne by your side."

"Dragons of the seven kingdoms of the north fail to remember that we still hold some form of human blood. Whether we choose to admit it. Our people prefer to live in our human form when we could just as easily curl up in our Dragon form in caves like the olden days. Fascinating, really."

Rowen never thought of it. She did envy the Dragons for being able to shift into both their bestial and human form with ease, when she was stuck in her human form.

"Doesn't change the fact that I am more human than Dragon. And, that will never change."

"Perhaps. But who cares what anyone thinks?"

Lawson laced his fingers into her hair and pulled her up to face him. A deep kiss awakened her body in ways that she'd never known before coming to Withrae.

When they parted, Rowen looked deep into his eyes. Could he make it work? He knew nothing of her ability to prophesize. Perhaps it was time to tell him.

"Lawson," Rowen whispered.

"Yes, my love."

"We've managed to keep our relationship a secret for almost a month."

"We have. Clever, aren't we?"

Rowen pursed her lips. Cleverer than you think.

"Indeed," Rowen said, mustering the courage to say what was on her mind. "But, do you have any secrets you wish to tell me?"

"Many," he said. "But there are some things best left unsaid, and some secrets that protect my kingdom."

Rowen sat up. "I see," she said.

"Why? Do you have secrets?"

Shaking her head, Rowen fixed the collar of his shirt and smoothed his burgundy vest. It seemed that she would take the truth of her machinations to her death bed. "None. You know all there is to know about me."

"Ah, but there is one thing I do not know. One thing that will be our only obstacle when we make our plans for marriage known."

Alarmed, Rowen's eyes widened. "And, what is that?"

He stroked her cheek, lingering on the spot where her bruise was fading.

"The truth of your origins," he said, and Rowen tensed. "I'd very much like to know who your father is."

My father? Rowen shook her head. He wondered the one thing she'd been searching for answers to all her life. She'd thought of him many times throughout her childhood, but no one had ever asked her about him.

"He's dead. Why does it matter?"

"Maybe it doesn't. Don't you ever wonder who he was?"

Rowen's shoulders slumped. "He's a mystery to me."

"But, you had to ask your mother about him. Aren't you a little curious?"

"He was a human," Rowen said, narrowing her eyes as she recalled how her mother described him. "Handsome, with eyes so gray that they were almost white."

"Like yours," Lawson said.

Nodding, Rowen went on. "He was charming and as my grandmother would say, he bewitched my mother and made her act recklessly. She risked everything to run away with him. She left her family and a chance to be royalty behind. To chase after a human that did nothing but break her heart."

"She loved him."

Like I love you, Lawson. Rowen thought of the moment she realized that Lawson had stolen her heart in the same way she'd dreamed of her mother's heart being stolen. Now that she knew what love looked like, she was certain that her mother never shared those feelings with her stepfather. She'd been promised to a king, fell for a human of no noble birth, and settled for a duke.

She could have done worse.

Rowen cupped Lawson's face in her hands. She'd reached high, and claimed royalty for her own. Could she reveal to him that that was her plan all along?

Her stepfather was wrong about most of the names he called her. But, ambitious and manipulative were the only true ones he'd ever used. The innocence of Rowen's face hid her many truths, and her plan to climb the ranks had worked.

Now, if only she could keep her prince, and her head.

"To think, your mother could be a queen now if she hadn't left."

"My mother and I are the same in many ways," Rowen said. "We'd do anything for love."

Lawson stroked her cheek with his thumb. "You know I'll never break your heart, don't you?"

Smiling, Rowen nodded and closed her eyes against the feel of his touch. "You better not."

He pulled her in for a kiss. Their lips touched and his hands slid up her dress to grab her naked thighs.

Locked in the kiss, Rowen's eyes widened. He'd never touched her that way, and while exciting, she feared where this level of intimacy was going.

His tongue parted her lips and eagerly, almost desperately, he worked to unlace the strings at the back of her dress.

"Lawson," Rowen said. "I can't right now. I must get back. Macana has an errand for me. I can't miss it. She's already suspicious of me." She hated lying to him, bit didn't like where he was taking things.

He grinned and lifted her into the air. "You have time," he said, and led her to one of the sofas against the far wall.

Rowen laughed nervously and used her hands to steady him. "I don't, my love. But, soon, I will."

Ignoring her, Prince Lawson parted her legs and gave her a wink. "Come now, darling. Let's have some fun. We should celebrate our love."

Something stirred within her belly, warming her from the inside out. It was shocking, almost making her cry out.

Time seemed to stand still. The drapes that had been flapping with the morning breeze at the windows behind them froze in midair. A whisper swept through the room, vexing her. She couldn't make out what it said, but it was clear that the prince hadn't heard it. He stared at her, and in an instant, the color drained from his face as Rowen lifted her other hand and touched his cheek.

It was purely instinctual, and satisfying.

The warmth she'd felt was replaced with a cold so bitter that it reminded her of the feel of the pond water just before winter transformed it into ice.

All emotion drained from the prince's face and he was left slack-jawed, staring at her with empty eyes.

"Prince Lawson? Are you okay?"

He didn't reply. He simply stared at her, as if in a trance.

The whisper filled her eyes again, and she struggled to make out what it said.

Rowen spoke calmly and clearly. "Let go of my wrist."

The prince snatched his hand away as if it were on fire. Still, she cupped his cheek and held his gaze.

Licking her lips, Rowen thought of what she should say. What she should do? This power was fleeting and she hadn't learned to master it yet.

"You will let me go. And, you will tell your father of our plans for marriage tonight."

Lawson nodded. "I will let you go. I will tell my father of our plans for marriage. Tonight."

"Holy light and fire," Rowen whispered.

Rowen let go of him and took a step back, stunned by what just happened. Her power was getting stronger.

The blood rushed back to her body, and the whispers faded into her head. Fear flooded her mind once more, as she waited for the prince to realize what had happened and to punish her for it.

Once released, Prince Lawson didn't seem to have any recollection of what just happened. He turned away from Rowen without another word and sat at his desk to return to whatever work he'd been doing prior to her arrival.

"You better get to Macana before you're late. I'll see you at the feast."

Rowen swallowed and nodded. Heart racing, mind frantic with ideas, she hurried to leave his room. She closed the door behind her and exhaled.

Outside in the hallway, she was left feeling dirty, and afraid. She didn't like where Lawson had tried to take their relationship. It could have sullied his desire to commit to her.

But, greater still, magic was forbidden.

Outlawed.

She bit her bottom lip and sucked in a worrisome breath.

She'd just bewitched someone... a prince. The punishment for that was certain death.

Rowen hurried to finish her errand, but the fact remained. She was stacking up enough broken laws to die several deaths.

CHAPTER NINE

TWO BLOODY DAYS. THAT'S HOW long Elian had been waiting for a competent scribe to show up.

Siddhe, for all her other talents, was frankly useless when it came to figuring out if an applicant was truly qualified. To be fair, Elian conceded that her failure was probably due to the fact she was a mermaid and had never learned nor had any use for reading or writing.

The third day in port found him twitchy and anxious to hire the next dunderhead that walked into his cabin and weigh anchor. The Wandering Star was never meant to bob dumbly on the water, safely tied up in dock. She was at her best slicing the waves with her hull while her sails fought to harness the wind. She was meant for action, just like him.

Still, when Siddhe warily poked her head into his cabin and announced there was a youth there to apply for the position of scribe, Elian curbed his restless energy and allowed him in.

The young man entered, giving Siddhe as wide a berth as possible while passing her in the doorway. He was tall and well-built, but not bulky, which was good. Men who were top-heavy from brawn or belly had worse balance on a rolling ship. The youth's movements were strong but relaxed. Dark hair and eyes, and thank the gods no freckles or spots like Cook. The bronze color of his skin looked like the effect of the sun rather than parentage. That was good as well, for anyone who lived on a ship needed skin that could withstand sun and wind, turning brown and tough instead of red and brittle.

Elian waited until the young man had come to stand before him, hands respectfully clasped behind his back. The sound of ticking from his pocket watch filled the silence of the room.

Time. It was the one treasure he could not steal.

Yet.

"Your name," he finally ordered after waiting just long enough for the other man to shift his weight in the first signal of nervousness.

"Gavin of Bristan, sir." There was a slight hesitation in his voice.

"No surname?"

"None given to serfs, sir."

Elian nodded once in acknowledgement. "How'd you get from serf to scribe?"

"My mam and pap saw that I had my head in the clouds more than hands on the plow. The priest found I could remember and recite the holy texts after hearing them just once. Since I was a lazy good-for-nothing around the farm, my mam and pap agreed to let the priest sponsor me to the temple school. Ten years of nose-to-parchment, another two apprenticing for a right bastard, three as a broke journeyman under a foxed master, and here I finally am. Free to choose my fate with my master scribe seal and nothing to lose."

Elian leaned back in his chair. The youth's bold words and cocky grin set his teeth on edge. It was like being with a chatty version of Siddhe. He wasn't sure if he could handle two of them. The ship rolled to the left, reminding him she was getting impatient to be off. Beggars, it appeared, couldn't be choosers.

"You're aware that I'm no... ah... commercial merchant?" he asked.

Gavin's grin flashed white against his sun-dark skin. "Knew it the moment I set eyes on the mermaid. But, I still walked in your door, didn't I?"

"You might still walk out with my boot up your arse, boy."

"Then, you'd be kicking out the best damn memory transcriber you ever crossed paths with."

"The best, eh?"

"Aye, sir. The very best."

"Prove it."

Gavin's grin slipped to a smile, and then a frown as he concentrated. Elian realized what he was doing and closed his eyes as well, summoning up the memory of a complex sales negotiation he had done two weeks prior regarding a cargo of spices that he had taken off some Harrovian merchant vessels.

He counted five heartbeats after the memory had played out fully, then opened his eyes.

Gavin was back to grinning.

"Fifty-one sacks of cedamom bark sold at thirty-two pence per pound, with each sack weighing ten pounds, give or take two ounces. Three barrels of pepperwine, aged ten years, sold at ninety pence per chalice, with each chalice equaling exactly one-third of a Harrovian commercial pitcher. Six sacks of margithyne sold at twenty-one pence per ounce, with each sack weighing two pounds, give or take one ounce. Payment terms are half upon acceptance of price terms and half upon delivery."

Elian's lower lip twitched. He couldn't help being slightly impressed. The young man didn't even wait for any reaction before continuing.

"I've got all the histories of all the kingdoms, tribes, and races. I read and write in seven languages – but, don't let that dissuade you if it's not enough. I'm teaching myself another two right now in my spare time, which, incidentally, I hope to have less of once you hire me. I'm rune-coder, bookkeeper, and draftsman."

He apparently ran out of things to say after that, and Elian began to teach him the language of silence.

"You talk a lot," Elian remarked finally. "The last man who had this job talked a lot, too. In fact, couldn't keep his trap shut."

"Don't worry about me, sir," Gavin said earnestly. "I'm no fool. I know when words need to be used and when they should be kept secret."

"Let us hope so." Elian sighed and shook his head. "Otherwise, you might find this job simply... sucks the life out of you."

The young man didn't miss the meaning gleam in the captain's eyes, and it was gratifying to see his Adam's apple bob up and down.

"So, does this mean I have the position?"

Elian had to admire the boy's boldness in the face of his fear.

"For now."

"Thank you, sir! You won't regret this."

The older man laughed humorlessly. "Aye, but you might... and probably will."

Siddhe strode in the moment Gavin left.

"Him?" The tone of her voice finished her sentence and added nearly a paragraph more on her opinion.

Elian pinched the bridge of his nose. Between the two of them, he'd go mad before he got to Withrae, let alone found the Red Dragon.

Siddhe sighed noisily, understanding his silence for assent, then turned and left to go settle the new scribe in and get the ship ready to depart.

By supper, they'd be riding out with the tide, on the way to Withrae.

He didn't know what he was supposed to be looking for in Withrae, but Cota hadn't let him down yet. He would find it, or it would find him.

And, then, he'd be one step closer to finding the Red Dragon and the treasure of time.

CHAPTER TEN

THE CENTRAL CHANDELIER IN THE center of the main ballroom of Withrae Castle lit the entire room with its many candles and hanging crystals. The king and queen of Withrae stood at the end of the hall, on a platform where their thrones were set. Prince Lawson and Prince Rickard were nowhere to be seen, but it wasn't surprising for them to arrive later than the guests.

Rowen and Brea stood at the back of Princess Noemie's procession, dressed in gowns designed and crafted by the master clothier. On either side of them was a crowd of noblemen, foreign dignitaries, and visiting royalty.

Rowen's eyes lit up when she saw a familiar face.

"Mother," she mouthed, smiling at her mother who stood at the front of the crowd in a red gown. There could have been no greater surprise than this. The fact that her stepfather was absent only brought more joy to her heart.

Whatever Prince Lawson had in mind for after the party couldn't compare to seeing her mother. Giddy with excitement, she followed the princess, eager to pull her mother aside and talk about all that she'd accomplished in just weeks of being at court.

The princess and her ladies walked to the area around the thrones, and the musicians changed their tune.

"Let's dance," Brea said, taking Rowen by the hand.

Rowen shook her head, paling at the thought. She took her hand back. "That's quite all right. You dance. I want to speak to my mother."

Brea's eyes lit up and she looked to the crowd. "What? She's here? Show me. I'd like to meet her."

"Certainly," Rowen said and with a bow to the princess, they headed into the crowd.

The noblemen of court parted a path for Rowen and Brea, yet made sure to cast their charming smiles. Ignoring them, Rowen's eyes went to her mother's. The duchess looked as regal as ever, and as beautiful as Rowen remembered. Her mahogany hair was worn long down her back, a faint glow of gold coming from the strands and the golden scales that ran up and down her exposed arms and neck.

"Darling," Lady Nimah said, holding her hands out.

Rowen slipped her hands into her mother's grasp and beamed when Lady Nimah pulled Rowen into an embrace and kissed her on the cheek.

"Are you well? You're too thin. Have they been feeding you?"

Laughing, Rowen nodded. "Yes. Of course. They feed us all the time. I can't remember the last time I actually felt hunger."

"Good," Lady Nimah said with a smile that warmed Rowen's heart. Her aura changed everything, and made the worries of the day fade into nonexistence. Just from the embrace alone, Rowen felt as though everything would be all right, that the world would be kind and never betray her. A piece of her wanted to leave and return home with her mother right away. If only they could run away together and be free of their duties and their past.

"Well, we have much to catch up on," Lady Nimah said.

"We do, but Mother," Rowen said, and placed a hand on Brea's shoulder. "This is my friend, Lady Brea of Red Shire."

Lady Nimah gave a slight bow of her head and Brea dipped into a curtsy.

"Duchess, it is a pleasure to meet you. Your daughter has spoken so highly of you and your beauty," Brea said.

"Lovely to meet you as well, Lady Brea. But, if you don't mind, I'd like to speak to my daughter alone."

Brea nodded and took a step away. "Of course." She turned to Rowen. "Don't think you're getting out of dancing tonight, young lady."

Rowen shook her head, laughing as Brea left to return to the other ladies-in-waiting. Hooking arms, Rowen and her mother left the crowd to a quiet spot near the entrance to the ballroom.

"So, is everything truly going well? I worry about you. Court can be a dangerous place."

Sighing, Rowen leaned against a pillar and looked her mother in the eyes. "Honestly, I am terrified. I've been having these dreams about being hanged. I think Macana knows something," she whispered.

Lady Nimah's brows furrowed, creasing her olive-colored skin. "Macana? What makes you think that?"

Rowen narrowed her eyes. "She is always watching me, and she's been asking questions lately. She doesn't hawk anyone else the way she does me."

"Well, I wouldn't worry about her. She's just a chaperone. Nothing more."

"I know. But, there is something about her. Just earlier, she grabbed me by my neck and threatened me."

"What?" Lady Nimah hissed. "How dare she put her hands on you? That is not like her at all. I know her."

"She did, and it's been bothering me all day."

"And the prince? How are things going there?"

A smile lifted the corners of Rowen's mouth. "That is the one thing that has gone right. He is smitten, and wants to marry me. But, he hasn't found a way to make it happen yet."

Lady Nimah stroked Rowen's hand. "Dear girl, that is a minor setback. He is the crown prince, his father is older than dirt, and it is only a matter of time before he becomes king. Who makes the rules then? The king. You just have to be patient."

"I know. But, I have this sinking feeling that something is going to go wrong. The prophecy worries me to no end. I have to find a way to thwart that fate." Rowen frowned. "I bet your husband could care less if I die, as long as his station is elevated."

"Nonsense. He isn't that cruel. If you die, there will be no elevation. He wants you to succeed."

Rowen stared at the crowd. "At least if I am successful, he'll no longer have any control over me."

"Darling, look at me."

Rowen looked at her mother and forced a smile.

"When you are queen, the only man that can ask anything of you is your husband. Prince Lawson, what is he like? Is he kind to you?"

"Kinder than any man has ever been."

Lady Nimah tilted her head. "You actually love him, don't you?"

Rowen stood up straight. "You can tell just from looking at me?"

With a laugh, Lady Nimah wrapped an arm around Rowen's shoulder and turned her toward the thrones at the other end of the ballroom. "No, darling. I've been in love once before, and I can see it in your eyes. There is no mistaking that look. Now, what better end to your stepfather's scheme than to be queen to the man you love?"

A hush filled the room as soldiers and guards burst through the doors behind them. The musicians stopped playing, and everyone stopped dancing to behold the soldiers whose swords were drawn as if ready for battle.

The grips of terror wrapped itself around Rowen's throat as she and her mother turned to them. Whatever had happened, had to be serious. The guards would have never burst into a formal event.

Rowen stepped aside to make room for them to pass. When the captain of the guards lowered his eyes to Rowen's face and pointed his sword's point at her, her blood turned cold and her body stiffened.

"Lady Rowen Glenick," he said, his deep voice booming and echoing off the walls of the ballroom.

Shaking, Rowen placed her hand on her chest. At first, the word stuck to the back of her throat and she had to swallow to bring it forth. "Me?"

"You're Lady Rowen Glenick, are you not?"

"I...I am." Rowen looked from her mother, to the crowd of staring faces, and back to the captain. "Is there something amiss?"

The captain of the guards grabbed her by her hand and yanked her toward him.

"What is it?" Rowen asked, her voice rising with anxiety.

This cannot be happening. It has to be another dream.

"Don't pretend as if you don't know," he growled. His eyes, fierce with rage left her face and looked to the crowd. "This woman is charged with treason."

Lady Nimah stepped forward, standing in between him and Rowen. "Whatever for, Mickleson? I am sure that whatever it is can be explained. You do not have to handle my daughter in such a vicious manner."

Mickleson shot her a glare, one that erased all thoughts that she would be able to talk her way out of this ordeal. "On the contrary, Duchess. Your daughter deserves worse."

"What for?"

"For killing the prince."

Everything went silent for Rowen in that moment. The outrage from the crowd fell into the background as his words resonated in her head, leaving her frozen in disbelief.

No. Her stomach dropped. No.

"Take her," Mickelson ordered.

Those words set her fate in stone. Her heart lurched and a cry escaped her mouth. Eyes burning with tears, she grabbed Captain Mickleson's collar.

She was too afraid to ask the question that burned inside her head. But, she had to know. As did everyone in attendance. Their heated stares burned into her, and the sound of her fiercely beating heart filled her ears.

"Which one?" she asked.

"Prince Lawson," he said.

Prince Lawson's face flashed before her eyes and she lost her balance, though Mickleson still held her tightly by the arm.

"No." Her entire world fell around her and all she could see were lights.

The room spun, her stomach twisted, and before she could form a goodbye to her mother, she was marched from the ballroom never to return.

CHAPTER ELEVEN

THE PRISON DOORS SLAMMED SHUT, and Rowen was left alone with her shock and tears. Darkness smothered her from all sides, and a damp chill in the air stung her bare arms as she looked out the prison tower's open window to the snowcapped mountains of Withrae. The smell of mold and urine was only camouflaged by the stronger smell of the coming storm.

Sleet fell in straight lines of translucent sheets, bringing more wind into her small cell with it.

Her home was a place of bitterness, but Rowen preferred it and its warm fires to that dingy prison. Withrae prison was set off of the castle grounds on a nearby mountain-top that experienced a year-long winter.

If she wanted to jump, she could, but even if she were able to shift into a dragon, she'd be shot with an enchanted bolt the moment she stood before the open window.

That was a known fact.

Still, the idea was tempting.

She had no direction, no idea how to cope, and so, she sat on the floor and curled her legs into her chest. Her gown's skirts were all she had to warm herself, and her tears froze to her face as quickly as they fell.

Prince Lawson. Her champion. Her love. The fate of the kingdom.

He was gone.

It wasn't possible. How could this happen after all of her planning, after all of their dreams for a life together? It seemed as though the luck Rowen had depended on all of her life had run out, abandoning her to a fate she'd seen but chose to tempt.

She squeezed her eyes shut. She should have escaped when she had the chance. Now, all was lost and she feared what was to come.

The noose. She knew that was her end. She just didn't want to believe it. Now, she had no choice. Treason was a hefty offense, one that came with not only death, but torture.

Rowen's stomach flipped and she gagged back vomit at the notion of suffering at the hands of the prison torturer. Though nobility were exempt from certain methods, there were others that would make any prisoner confess to crimes they'd never imagined.

With a whimper, she buried her face into her dress and clenched her hands into fists.

Think, Rowen. Think. There has to be a way out of this.

No one told her what to do if she were caught, and no one dared to think the prince would die.

The creaking of the prison door drew her attention, and as she turned around her face paled. Standing in the doorway with a prison guard was Prince Rickard. He spoke a few words that Rowen couldn't make out to the guard and the burly Dragon nodded and left them alone.

"A smarter girl would have married my brother and then killed him. But, no one ever accused you of being a great thinker. Still, that's what I'd have done if I were a social climber with no other prospects," Rickard said.

"What do you want?"

His lips curled into a snarl as he stood before her at the bars. "Look at you. Already breaking, are we?" He lowered himself to her level and examined her face. "I thought you would at least last an hour."

Tears burned her eyes, and Rowen repeated herself, clenching her teeth. "What do you want?" She should have known. He came to gloat when he should be grieving. That was his way. The way of an opportunistic maniac.

Rickard's shirt was damp, clinging to his chest and untucked. The sleeves were rolled up to his elbows. Dark hair hung long around his face, wet and slick as if he'd ran through the sleet to reach the tower.

Rowen took a closer look, bringing her face toward the bars. She narrowed her eyes at seeing that his eyes were indeed red, and swollen.

Maybe he had shed a few tears of his own.

"If you loved him, why did you kill him?"

Rowen grabbed the bars and her brows lifted. This was her chance to plead her case. He had more power than most and could help her. Perhaps she could use his attraction for her to free herself.

"Prince Rickard, I didn't. I swear it. On all things holy and full of light, you know I loved him. And, he loved me. Why would I do such a thing? I would have done anything for Lawson."

Shaking his head, Rickard licked his lips. With a sigh, he sat on his bottom and stared at her. "That's what I am here to find out. I wanted to talk to you first, before the law gets involved, before the prison torturer gets his blood-crusted hands on you."

"But, I didn't do it," Rowen said, her shoulders slumping. "Please. Believe me."

He leaned forward, his eyes narrowing into slits of bright blue that glowed in the dark like a cat's. "And, no one will ever believe you. Unless you admit to it. Understand?"

Appalled, Rowen's jaw dropped.

"Do you understand what I am saying to you, Rowen?"

Rowen shot to her feet. Her voice rose as her cheeks reddened. "I will not! I didn't kill your brother, and I will never say that I did. To even advise me to do such a thing just makes me hate you even more."

For a moment, Rickard was silent and watched her from the floor. Then, he lowered his head.

"They will want a confession, Rowen."

"They will not get it from me."

"Then, they will torture you for it," Rickard said, and pushed himself up to his feet.

He gave her one last look and reached out to her. Midway to the bars, he stopped and pulled his hand back, vexing her in more ways than one.

Rowen couldn't let him leave. Even if she did hate him, he was her only hope. She held onto the bars. "Help me, Rickard. Please."

He shrugged. "What do you think I'm trying to do?"

Rowen couldn't formulate a coherent statement. Rickard's question left her speechless, her mind in chaos.

Once he left, Rowen was left more confused than when she arrived.

Rickard knows I didn't do this. She covered her mouth. But, he knew something. She had to find out what that was.

A sinking feeling worse than the thought of losing her love washed over her. She looked out to the open window and stepped as far toward it as she dared, her skirts flapping in the wind that grew fiercer.

Looking out to the midnight purple sky, she wondered, who killed her prince?

CHAPTER TWELVE

THE BROKEN GLASS FROM A mirror embedded itself into Rowen's pale flesh. She winced, but kept her mouth shut as she watched her stepfather storm from the sitting room and into the wintry night.

Once he was gone from sight, Rowen and her mother rushed to one another.

"I'm sorry," Rowen's mother, Nimah said. "His temper gets out of hand."

"More often than naught," Rowen said as she fought back tears and wrapped her arms around Nimah's neck. She buried her face in her mother's dark mass of silky hair and breathed in her scent one last time.

There was no room for a half-blood in the manor anymore. She'd known that since she was old enough to realize that the Dragons looked at her differently. Eighteen years of life amongst her mother's people did nothing to change their minds. Even if her mother was the Duchess of Harrow, it did nothing to remove the taint of the human blood that ran through Rowen's veins.

Now, she was uprooted from her home once again and was about to be sent off on a dangerous mission to elevate the entire family.

Money and power were all that her stepfather, the Duke, cared about. Now that Rowen was old enough to contribute, her time had come. If her beauty couldn't pull them from the poverty her stepfather's dealings were leading them toward, nothing would.

"Don't apologize," Rowen whispered. "You did nothing wrong, Mother."

Nimah pulled away, and held Rowen out at arm's-length. "I should have left with your father long ago. Staying here has only embittered the both of us."

Rowen looked into her mother's golden eyes that matched her long wavy hair. How many times has Rowen begged the gods to allow her to look like her mother? Being half human muddied her features. There was no shimmer or glow to her skin like the other full-blooded Mount Withrae Dragons. Only a pale peaches and cream that made her stand out like a weed in a bed of flowers.

"The Dragons would have disowned you and the humans would have killed us for stepping foot on their soil."

Nimah wiped a tear from the corner of her eye. "I dare say that I don't care. Let me at least come with you to the castle until you get settled. The king will allow it. We are old friends."

Tensing, Rowen shook her head and took a step away. "No. I must go alone. We both know that. I have to do this on my own." She grabbed her cloak from the hooks on the wall. A quick glance at her hands revealed that her wounds from the glass had healed within seconds. The blood still stained her palms, however.

"I have to go, Mother. It's time."

Nimah wrung her hands, looking to the open doorway as a chilly wind swept in. "Please, be careful. Life at court is not like at home."

"Is it better?" Rowen asked.

Nimah pursed her lips. "It is what you make it. But, everyone will have their eyes on you, and if you mess up our plan, there will be no escaping punishment."

"I know," Rowen said. "But, I am afraid."

"Do what your stepfather says, and we will all benefit from your success."

"But, what if I fail?"

"Then, Rowen," Nimah said, her shoulders slumping. "We will be ruined."

The sounds of screaming filled Rowen's ears when she woke from her dream. Where were the prophecies now? They'd been replaced with painful memories. It wasn't fair. How could her power abandon her now, at her darkest hours?

Darkness seemed to be Rowen's only friend as she wasted away in the prison tower, awaiting a friendly face, the return of Prince Rickard, or her legal counsel. The waiting left her on edge, so much so that she spent her days seated on the floor in front of the window, watching the sky, the snowy mountains, and the patch of woods that she could make out far away.

Then, there were the screams. They came and went, sometimes for hours. Sometimes all night. No matter the duration, they made Rowen's skin crawl and the hairs on her neck and arms stand on end.

Cries of agony and anguish echoed throughout the prison, and there was no escaping it, no matter how hard Rowen pressed the palms of her hands to her ears. It was a constant reminder that soon her own screams would resonate throughout the prison.

Prince Lawson was dead.

Her eyes welled with tears. She'd thought that she had no more left to shed, but they kept coming, rolling down her dirty cheeks as she sobbed into her hands. They'd only known each other for a few weeks, but that time stolen to be together had given her purpose and had made life bearable. His smile lingered in her mind, and then visions of a cold lifeless body took over and sent her into an abyss of grief.

When the door behind her opened, hope swelled in her heart.

She scrambled to her feet and turned to face whatever visitor had come for her.

It wasn't a friendly face, but a stranger. Hesitant, Rowen watched the tall, older Dragon stand before her cell and fold his thick arms before him.

"Smeathe," he said with a slight nod toward her that made his long, stringy gray and black hair fall over his shoulders. "Mr. Smeathe. I'll be your legal counsel in the charges of treason and murder."

Rowen rushed to the bars. "Where is my mother? Is she safe?"

"Yes, the Duchess is still in the palace awaiting your trial. She petitions to visit you every day."

Relieved that she hadn't been arrested as well, Rowen exhaled. "Good. But, why won't they let her come to me?"

"The king's orders. No one is to come to you except for myself and the royal family."

"Princess Noemie? Has she said anything about this?"

Mr. Smeathe shook his head. "She has been grieving in her private quarters."

"I see," Rowen said. She flickered a hopeful look up to him. "Listen. I didn't do it. I assure you there has been a misunderstanding. I hadn't seen Prince Lawson since the morning of the birthday celebration."

"So, you did see him that day?"

Taken aback, Rowen was a bit flustered by the question. She snapped her mouth closed and stared at him, wondering if she should reveal the truth of her relationship with Prince Lawson.

"You saw him the day of the incident?"

"What is the incident? What happened to Prince Lawson?"

Mr. Smeathe gave her a look that told her that he wouldn't believe anything she said. He already thought she was guilty. This was all for show.

"Tell me," she said despite knowing that he looked at her like the person responsible.

"Poison," Mr. Smeathe said.

Poison? Rowen didn't need any disturbing images to add to her nightmares, but picturing Lawson suffering from a deadly poison cut into her heart.

"Will you answer my question now, Miss? Did you see the prince on the night of the incident?"

Rowen glared at him. "You're not my legal counsel, are you?"

The corners of Mr. Smeathe's mouth twitched, but he kept his composure. With a nod of his head, he answered her question.

Defeated, Rowen gave up and went back to her spot by the window.

"Let's drop all pretenses now, young lady. Tell me how you did it and why."

"I'll tell you nothing. The other ladies-in-waiting can account for my whereabouts."

He lifted a brow and his mouth twisted.

That wasn't reassuring. Rowen stood back on her heels and her shoulders slumped. "What is it?"

Mr. Smeathe stared at her with cold, dark eyes. "The ladies-in-waiting are all testifying against you."

"No," Rowen said. She'd have sat back down if there had been a chair. She couldn't let this stranger see her sitting on the floor like a peasant.

"Yes. You haven't a chance but to tell us the truth. Maybe we can avoid sending you to Jahns."

Rowen didn't ask, but she had a feeling it was someone she didn't want to see. "Wait," Rowen said, pressing her fingertips to her temples. Picturing Ishma and the others sneering at her while she fought for her life was too much. "That cannot be. They have no right. Whatever testimony they plan to give is a lie."

"They are not the ones on trial. You are. Let's not forget that."

Rowen opened her mouth. Nothing came out but a painful wheeze. She coughed and turned away, embarrassed by the hacking sound she'd developed after days of being subjected to bitter cold and little food and water. When the coughing fit ended, Rowen wiped her mouth and stared out the window.

This was all surreal. If only she could wake up, she could sneak off to Lawson's quarters and give him the kisses and passion he desired the last time she saw him.

"You said the ladies-in-waiting are all testifying."

"That is correct."

"Even Lady Brea?" Saying the words cut deep into her already tender and broken heart. He'd already given his answer, but she needed to hear it again. She needed to prepare herself for the betrayal that was to come.

"Lady Brea has compelling eye-witness accounts against you. They will likely use her to solidify your sentence. Now, aren't you going to tell me everything so we can move this trial along?"

Rowen chewed her bottom lip and sucked in a breath of cold air. It was too much to take in. No one prepared her for this. Lady Brea had been prepared to help her escape if need be. Now, she was willing to aid in Rowen's execution. The notion embittered her in a way that took her sadness away. There was no room for sadness anymore.

"No," Rowen said. "Leave me."

"Suit yourself. They will hang you for this."

Rowen shot him a glare, her hands balled into fists as pain and rage filled her veins. "They can try."

CHAPTER THIRTEEN

ROWEN COULD TASTE FREEDOM AS she was taken from the prison tower and led down the stone mountain path to her trial. The taste was bitter, because she was not free. Her arms were bound before her with ropes, and she'd been clothed in a plain gray gown that reached her leather shoes.

Her ordeal was just beginning.

It had been nearly another week since she'd seen or spoken to anyone other than the prison guard who brought her bread and water. That morning, she was allowed to clean herself with an old rag and a pail of cool water. There was nothing she could do about her hair, but rake through the tangles with her numb fingers.

Cold and shivering, she could barely keep up with the guards that led her down the icy path. Snow fell from the dark sky of dawn, and Rowen's arms were tight with gooseflesh. The howling of the wind had become a lullaby. Now, it wrapped around her and blew her dress out, nearly lifting her from the ground.

"Lucky Jahns didn't get his hands on you," Morse, the prison master that led the way said over his broad shoulder. He had a bald head and wore armor that had the Withrae crest on the left shoulder. "He'd have stripped that pretty flesh of yours right off the bones. Killing the prince. They'd have impaled a peasant for much less. And, you get off without so much as the sting of a whip. Damned lucky, you are."

Rowen ignored him. She was tired of hearing about luck. Her feet were sore and her toes were frostbitten, but she kept her head held high and her eyes ahead. Weary and full of anxiety, Rowen was led through the prison gates, and out onto the road. A black horse and tumbril awaited her, to transport her to the Withraen courthouse. Without a word, Morse lifted her from the ground and set her inside the wooden tumbril.

She glared at him as he sat across from her with his sword drawn and resting in his lap.

He gazed at her thoughtfully and folded his arms across his breastplate. His gaze rested on her bosom, and a leer came to his face. "Shame," he said under his breath.

Rowen turned away in her seat with a huff. Her cheeks burned as she fixed her eyes on the world outside. The snow-crusted ground and white trees broke way for a frozen river that ran along the road. The mountainous area opened to flat meadows and fields of onions and winter vegetables.

It would probably be the last time she'd see the countryside again. It was sobering to realize that these may very well be her last hours.

Only a prophet can change their fate. Rowen had her chance, and squabbled it away for the love of a man, the approval of her stepfather, and the security of her mother.

Were her motives so misguided?

The tumbril rolled down the mountain path toward the city, and Rowen prepared herself for the fight of her life, for her life.

ARRIVING TO THE courthouse was worse than Rowen expected. The quiet of the bumpy ride abruptly ended the moment the tumbril slowed to a stop in the square. The sky was overcast, the air thick with fog.

An angry mob waited for her, their voices rising to a deafening roar the moment she was spotted.

"There she is!"

"The prince killer!"

"Burn the half-blood scum!"

Those words shocked Rowen. She hesitated to move a muscle. Rowen looked to Morse, fearful that they would tear her limb-for-limb if they got their hands on her.

Morse noticed her pleaful look and chuckled. "Off we go, prince killer," he said, lifting her from the back of the tumbril by her armpits. He set her on the path from the stone road to the large building before her.

Hiding her fear for what lay ahead, Rowen sucked in a breath and quickened her stride. That didn't stop the angry citizens of Withrae from throwing things at her. Rotten food and rocks were pelleted at her head and she had to duck to avoid having anything hit her face.

She wanted to cry. They had it all wrong. But, Rowen forced the tears to stay back, and reached the safety of the main entrance all while people shouted obscenities at her and condemned her for killing their prince.

The names they called her would never be forgotten.

Though, her time to remember them was very short.

The courtroom fell silent as Rowen stepped inside. Though the protesters outside of the courthouse continued to yell, there was order inside. Nonetheless, she could tell by the looks on the audience's faces that they felt as strongly as those outside.

Their scornful scowls awaited.

They hated her.

Her heartbeat filled her ears, and the palms of her hands grew wet with sweat. This was it. Her last chance to prove herself innocent.

The king and queen weren't there, which wasn't surprising. They left these matters to the city judge. Princess Noemie hadn't shown up either. However, Prince Rickard, dressed in his formal attire, sat near the judge, his eyes watching her as she entered. His last words to her still left her confused, and seeing him there to watch her be sentenced to death was unnerving. Maybe he truly cared for her in his own way and would speak in her defense.

Rowen could only hope.

Swallowing, Rowen's eyes left Prince Rickard to behold Nemith, the Withraen judge. In his Dragon form, he took up most of the center of the room with his large body of black and gold. Large golden eyes watched her, unblinking, and cold. His head reached just inches from the top of the room which had a vaulted ceiling painted the same red as the rows of seats that went up and down the floor. No seat was empty on that day.

It seemed all of Withraen Castle court was present, watching, judging. They were stuffed in the seats, prepared for an entertaining ruling. If only there was one person there that was on her side. She knew little of how these proceedings went. One thing was known, not many prisoners were found innocent. Without legal counsel, Rowen knew her odds of getting out of this. She had yet to think of a strategy that might actually work.

All she had, was the truth.

She prayed that it was enough.

Rowen fought tears when she saw her mother raise her hand to draw her attention.

Mother. Rowen whimpered.

She had come. Rowen should have expected it. Her desire to have someone on her side fleeted. She hated to have her mother witness her sentencing. To think that she would never feel the comfort of her mother's embrace again broke her heart.

Rowen nodded to her and sucked in a cleansing breath.

She refused to cry in front of the court.

Morse led her to a wooden box with short sides so that everyone could see her, and a single door at the back. It stood in the center of the court, right before the Dragon. He turned the lock and stepped away, folding his arms across his chest and resuming a blank look.

Rowen leaned against the railing with both hands and stared at Brea with glossy eyes as they led her into the courtroom.

Brea avoided her gaze and kept her eyes down at the floor before her chair as she sat down.

"State your name."

"Lady Brea Rosewood."

"Lady Brea Rosewood, what happened the day of Prince Lawson's murder? You were with Lady Rowen for a greater part of it, correct?"

She nodded, and glanced at Rowen.

"Did Lady Rowen ever leave your side?"

"Yes," Brea said. She shifted in her seat.

"Tell me about that."

"She left Princess Noemie's dressing for a bit. I believe she was sent on an errand. But, we never talked about the princess' errands. Rowen was usually the lady that she chose for such things."

"Any other times?"

Rowen noticed how Brea hesitated to answer. She dared to hope that her best friend in the castle would not condemn her with lies or things she did not understand.

Brea's voice came out soft, and airy. "Yes."

"How many?"

Sighing, Brea closed her eyes. "Twice more that day."

"We are listening."

"We went with Macana into the city. Rowen left my side for a moment and visited the herb shop."

Nemith's gaze went to Rowen's. "Let the records show that Lady Rowen visited the herb shop, where the poison was surely purchased."

"How so? I didn't purchase anything! I only went inside to look while Macana purchased something. Why isn't she here?"

Nemith lowered his face to the box where Rowen stood. A low growl rumbled from his throat, signaling that this was not the trial she thought it was. She couldn't defend herself. The sentencing was already complete in the minds of the court and the judge.

"You will not talk out of turn again. Understood?"

Rowen tensed, and looked Nemith in the eyes.

Surprisingly, her fear had fleeted. They'd already made up their minds about her.

"I will speak the truth, if anyone wants to hear it," Rowen said through clenched teeth. Her heart pounded, and her hands shook with rage. "Prince Lawson loved me. We were going to be wed. I would have never dreamed of killing him. And, all you have are false claims and the testimonies of women that don't have a clue of what they are talking about."

Nemith snorted, a cloud of smoke puffing from his nostrils.

"I've made my decision," he said.

All eyes went to Rowen.

Before he could speak another word, Rowen lifted her bound hands and managed to get one fingertip placed onto his face. She narrowed her eyes, the whispers in her head chanting in a language she did not understand.

"I am innocent, and you know it. See?" Rowen asked, closing her eyes as she allowed her memories to be unlocked and shared with the Dragon judge.

All went silent and the world stilled as she showed him how much she cared for Lawson, and how she had been with the princess and Macana the entire day. Their time in Lawson's room flashed before her and the tears fell. There was nothing she could do to hold them back as the memories took over her entire mind and left her defenseless against her emotions.

The moment was brief, for Morse yanked her backward by her hair and pinned her to the ground.

The sounds of the courthouse returned to her at full force, leaving her disoriented as she stared at the ceiling trying to regain her senses.

"Witch!"

"Sorceress!"

Those words drifted into her ears and turned her blood cold.

The truth was out, and there was nothing she could do to take it back. Rowen struggled to sit up, but Morse's strong hands pinned her by the neck.

"Stay put," he growled.

Rowen tried to get a look at Nemith, desperate to hear the words that he believed her, that the truth was so clear that there was no doubt that she couldn't have killed Prince Lawson.

Instead, the shouts from the crowd filled the room, leaving nothing but cries of anger and demands that she be executed immediately.

"It's what we get for letting half-blooded humans into our borders. The filth of magic clings to you," Morse said. "And, you will pay for it."

"Let me go," Rowen said, as calmly as she could.

His grip on her neck tightened, cutting off her ability to take in a full breath.

"LET ME GO!"

With a roar, Rowen kicked him between the legs. He sucked in a grunt of pain and she shoved him off of her and a few feet across the wooden floor.

Flushed, Rowen scrambled to her feet.

The crowd hushed briefly, stunned by her show of strength.

She looked pass the crowd to Nemith.

"Tell me, judge. Will you condemn me for something you know I didn't do?"

Her eyes met Rickard's, who beheld her with a look of quiet awe. Back to Nemith's face, she waited, her chest heaving with the exertion of using her strength on Morse, and her breaths struggling to calm.

Nemith outstretched his wings and pointed one talon to the door.

"The gallows," he said in a voice that was tight with rage. "Take her. Now!"

So, Rowen thought, her shoulders slumping. She'd given it her all, and even exposed herself as a magic user.

This is it.

CHAPTER FOURTEEN

IT WAS RAINING WHEN THE Wandering Star finally approached Withrae. Elian stoically studied the sky, following the puffs and billows of the heavy grey clouds, blinking away the water as it fell into his eyes.

He could tell by the shifting light that this rain fell only offshore. Withrae itself would be dry. Depending on which way the wind changed in a few hours, the rain might move inland. He shrugged. Arriving half-wet, half-dry, and entirely itchy was not his favorite way to come into port, but he had done it before and would doubtless do it again.

Around him, the crew went about their tasks briskly. Elian restrained himself from smirking. Perhaps the rain was a blessing in disguise as it made them quicker and quieter, all the more eager to get into port and out of the wet.

He looked over to Siddhe where she crouched on the far end of the bowsprit. Cocoa-colored flesh, tight corset, and even tighter leather pants all worked to make her look like a goddess amongst men.

The wind whipped her hair until it thrashed like a wild creature caught on a hook. The salt water crashed and sprayed around her as the boat bucked and jumped on the waves. Through it all, she remained in perfect balance, though there was a restless energy that put a beautiful tension into the lines of her body.

She had no fear of falling into the ocean. Why would she fear going home? He knew it was what she most longed for, and he knew that as long as he lived, it was what she could never do.

"Bloody hell!" Gavin yelled from just behind him. "It's windier than a pack of farting monkeys up here!"

Elian closed his eyes and prayed for patience. Brilliant scribe. Remarkable memory transcriber. Utter and complete pain in his arse. The scale between practicality and murder teetered more precariously every day.

"Gor! Is that Siddhe? Isn't that a trick, eh? 'Look, mam, no ropes!'"

Was it too much to hope for a rogue wave to sweep him away?

"What's that long, pointy beam thing she's perched on called, anyway?"

The scales tipped precipitously toward murder.

THEY BROKE THROUGH the wall of fog and drizzle an hour later. The wind in the harbor was sharp, cold, and strangely acrid. Elian blinked to make sure the clouds were not playing a trick on him. No, that was definitely smoke rising from the dockside quarter of Withrae. Not just one fire, either, and not just in that quarter.

It was too late to come about and sail off. They were surrounded by chaotic boat traffic in the harbor. Besides, Cota had told him to come to Withrae, and he wasn't going to leave until he found the next part of the puzzle.

Siddhe slid back down the bowsprit to join him on the prow.

"Rioting," she said, the gills on her neck fading as the sea water on her flesh dried.

He nodded to accept the verdict of her keen eyesight and hearing. She was better than any spyglass because she understood what she saw and could think.

"No rumor of it when we left last time?" he asked.

Siddhe shook her head. "No more than the usual blood muttering."

"Full-blood, half-blood, so foolish. What's a human, then? No blood? All blood is red on the tip of a blade."

Siddhe looked at him curiously, and he realized he had let his bitterness slip out. He locked it away once more. It was nothing but ancient history. History he wished he could forget.

"I am different from you," she said, her expression carefully blank.

"Aye, but we're the same where it counts." He heard her inhale softly. "You don't need your blood to match to roll in the hay."

"I see," Siddhe said, nodding. She pursed her lips and turned on her heel and went to supervise the final tying off of the ropes and the rolling down of the gangplank.

His words stung her. Elian would have to deal with that later. Now, his eyes were fixed on the port ahead. He looked to the skies.

"I'm here," he whispered. "Now, what do you have for me."
It better be good.

CHAPTER FIFTEEN

"**I**T'S THE CROWN PRINCE," GAVIN announced breathlessly as he jogged up to Elian and Siddhe.

The captain frowned. He hadn't even noticed Gavin leaving the ship behind them as they cautiously made their way through the burning dockside quarter.

"He's dead."

"No point in a riot," Siddhe remarked. "Won't bring him back."

"He was murdered."

Siddhe shrugged to imply her point was still valid. Gavin looked crestfallen for a moment, then rallied.

"They're executing his killer today," he continued. "But, get this – Prince Lawson's killer is a girl!"

Elian stilled. "What did you say?"

Gavin nodded. "A girl. Apparently, she was his lover or something. Or claimed to be."

"But, why riot?" Siddhe persisted.

"Because she's not just a girl, she's a half-blood dragon. The full-blood dragons are clamoring for her head, and the half-bloods and humans see it as another example of the king's oppression of their rights."

"How exactly did you learn all this?" Elian asked, more to buy time for his mind to process all the ramifications of this information than because of any real interest in the kingdom's politics.

"I, erm, ran into a girl I, uh, used to know. She was a barmaid at the Four Goblets in Lidenhold. A friend of mine. Just a friend. A good friend."

Elian thought that any good friend of the lad's would have put him out of his misery long before then, but there was no accounting for people or taste.

Yet, the levity did nothing to shrug the strange weight off his heart.

A half-blood girl.

Thoughts and questions darted like a school of little silver fish through his mind, too quick and impossible to capture. The only thing he was certain of was an impulse to go see this girl, even if it was only to watch her die.

"Been a while since we've been to a good execution," Siddhe said.

He felt her gaze studying him as she unerringly guessed his thoughts. Gavin looked a bit green at the notion, but followed them as they trailed the crowds toward the gallows.

It would have been easy to push ahead through the throngs of people. But, the smooth skin of two humans and a mermaid were conspicuous enough in the sea of glowing complexions and shiny scales in the Withraen people.

Elian paid no heed to the royal stands or bright pennants flapping in the wind. It was all shine and show for the sake of pride, and the gods knew, he'd had stomached enough of 'noble pride' in his life.

"Oy, wotch it!"

Clamping down on his instinct to tense, he saw Siddhe do the same as a tall, burly woman pushed past them in the crowd. The visible scales on her skin meant she was a full-blood dragon, but not refined like the nobility, who had ridiculous rules about scales and skin.

What did scales or skin matter in the dark when your body moved in rhythm with the one you loved? Oh, wait, it mattered because stupidity didn't discriminate across blood.

He noticed Siddhe stiffen then instantly relax, even though her fingertips twitched reflexively. Still, he knew she was wise enough not to cause a scene in the midst of a crowd where even the half-blood dragon common maidens were sturdy enough to knock Gavin to the ground.

Like water finding its level, the crowd slowed and stopped, filling in all around the gallows, with a small rivulet of space opening up for the tumbril to move through. He could make out the waving feathers from the guards' helmets as he tracked the tumbril's progress, but the condemned girl was too short to be seen, even raised from the ground on the cart.

"Looks like half the kingdom's here," Gavin whispered excitedly.

Elian rolled his eyes. "Aye, and a right proper mess it'll be if half a kingdom of dragons decides to brawl in a city square."

Gavin sucked in a breath. The captain snorted. Let that be a lesson in gawking at a crowd without thinking of the risks and possibilities. A low roar rose up from the people as the tumbril clattered to a halt. Blood insults, jeers, and curses filled the air. Ugly sentiments for an ugly crime and ugly punishment.

It's not that he wasn't all for law and order–so long as the law didn't apply to him, and the order didn't get in his way. He'd handed out plenty of whippings for infractions by his crew. He'd dealt worse to traitors like Cook. But, he liked his justice to be one-to-one. One crime, one guilty party, one punisher, one punishment. A crowd like this had a tricky riptide of hate and violence running through it. It was too easy to be swept up and carried along.

A cluster of guards surrounded the prisoner as she made her way up the steps of the gallows, blocking the crowd's view of her. Elian absently toyed with the idea of experimenting and seeing if he could take in her soul from this distance. He'd never stilled time for this many people before, nor breathed in from this far. He might be able to do one or the other without consequence. But, both might leave him weak. Vulnerable. He'd have to trust Siddhe and Gavin to get him back to ship.

Siddhe stood calmly with her hand resting on the carved walrus bone hilt of the knife at her side. She'd have his back. He trusted her.

Gavin was bobbing up on his toes trying to get a better view of the gallows and lost his balance when he tried to scratch the back of his neck at the same time.

Elian sighed. Never mind.

The crowd let out a savage whoop when the guards parted to reveal the condemned girl.

Elian's heart gave a painful lurch.

Young. So young.

Too young. Terrified. That much was clear despite the girl's desperate attempts at dignity. A shaft of sun broke through the overcast skies and landed on her hair, turning prison-dirty blonde to shining gold and copper.

He released a breath he didn't even know he was holding.

The king's bailiff stepped forward and unfurled the scroll in his hands.

"Oyez! Oyez! Oyez! Right good dragons of Withrae, listen now to the word of your king, His Majesty King Thorne, full-blood dragon and gracious sovereign of this land."

He didn't need Siddhe's eyesight to see the girl's trembling. The muscles in his jaw hurt from clenching so tightly.

"For the crimes of high treason against king and country and the murder with malice aforethought of Crown Prince Lawson, Rowen Glenick, half-blood dragon of Harrow, is hereby sentenced to hang from the neck until dead."

A wave of dizziness washed over Elian, and he gasped as his line of sight went dark then shifted.

He stood upon the gallows, cold and shaking. The crowd was a blur behind unshed tears. Fear made every vein pulse pound with each frantic heartbeat. The ropes were scratchy, then too tight. It was hard to breathe, and the bottom of the platform hadn't even fallen out yet. Blink. The tears rolled down his cheeks, clearing his vision. Out of the sea of faces, one figure stood out. A grey-cloaked figure who raised his head and locked gazes with him.

He was staring at himself.

"Elian!" Siddhe hissed, the pain of her fingers digging into his arm bringing him back to the moment.

He blinked and raised his head to look at the girl on the gallows.

She looked right at him, and a startled expression of recognition flitted across her face.

Holy hells, this was why he had come to Withrae. The epiphany slammed into him. This girl was the next key to the map of the Red Dragon. In the back of his mind, he grumbled at Cota. Just for once, couldn't a vision be easy, like, say, going and buying a book or burning some herbs?

"We're going to steal her," he whispered, his lips barely moving, but knowing that Siddhe heard every word.

Her grip on his arm became excruciating. "You're mad."

He grasped Gavin's cloak and pulled the young man over. He spoke directly into Gavin's ear. "When I give the signal, you are going to run up and grab the girl, then hightail it back to the ship. Understood?"

Gavin gaped at him. "B-but, I'm a scribe!" he whimpered.

"Yeah, well, you're a bloody pirate now," Elian hissed. "Siddhe, you're with me."

"Wait, this is insane!" Gavin muttered. Siddhe looked both shocked and disgusted that for once, she agreed with the lad. Elian couldn't deny it, either, but it had to be done.

He tumbled through his thoughts, frantic for a ploy that stood even the slightest chance of working against a crowd of tens of thousands of full-blood and half-blood dragons, the full complement of the elite royal guard, and the royal family. Bugger his life.

The drumroll began. Time was up.

Elian summoned all his power and inhaled, inflating his lungs unnaturally until his ribs almost cracked from the strain.

The rope went around the girl's neck. She closed her eyes.

He threw his head back and roared.

From the bowels of his spirit, he spewed forth the thousand dark souls he had swallowed from a lifetime of dealing death. They shot into the air with black shrieks and foul shadows that blotted out the sky.

"Holy hells!" Gavin yelled.

"Fool! That's your signal!" Siddhe shouted, shoving the young man into the crowd.

The dark souls were enraged from their confinement in Elian's spirit. They swooped and dove down into the crowds, their shadowy forms going through body after body, leaving them to fall limp and dead to the ground as their numbers swelled.

All around him, there was the sound of shredding cloth as men and women shifted to their dragon forms and took to the skies, some to flee, others to breathe fire in an effort to fight the dark souls. They were no match for the unholy spirits, and the earth shook as dragons fell from the sky and crashed to the ground, crushing buildings, and splitting the stones of the grand marble plaza.

The royal stands had been emptied, the guards dragging the king and other nobles back into the safety of the palace. Soldiers from the elite royal guard rushed at Elian and Siddhe.

He could do little but hold his ground and gulp in great breaths. He felt empty, brittle, weak, as if his bones had been hollowed out and sinews stripped away. Tremors wracked his body as he swayed and stumbled like a newborn foal.

Siddhe paid him no mind, except to register where he was so that her swinging blades missed him as they sang their way through the air to sink into flesh. She danced around him in a whirl of death, subtly moving them foot-by-foot toward the far end of the square where escape might be possible.

The ground grew slick from the blood and gore spilled by Siddhe's double swords. He slipped, banging his knee against the stone as he tried to save himself from the fall and regain his footing.

"Bloody hell, and I mean that literally!" Gavin's voice was pitched high with pain.

Elian could barely lift his head to see that the scribe was half-dragging, half-being-carried by the girl. She looked dazed, as if she had been pushed past the threshold of abject terror and was now numb and mechanical. Good enough. He didn't need a hysterical female on his hands at the moment.

The dark souls were beginning to dissipate, their rage caught like smoke on the wind and pulled away from them, strand by strand. In a few more moments, they'd be gone, released from their earthly bondage and free to flee to the spirit world.

Speaking of fleeing, Elian was relieved to find they were at the end of the square. He even allowed himself just the faintest bit of hope that they would actually make it back to the ship alive.

Until the giant carcass of a dragon landed before them, blocking off their escape route. Just before everything went black, Elian thought sourly once more of how he wished that just once, this quest involved sitting in a tavern with a tankard of ale and a nice, hot bowl of stew.

IN THE END, it was Gavin's... special friend, the barmaid who saved them. She had followed them to the square, and when they were trapped by the fallen dragon, pulled them to hide out in a tavern in the square. She led them through a complex network of cellars that connected the various taverns in the city until they reached the docks. The riots along the water's edge allowed them to almost strut back onto the ship. In a bloodied, smoke-stained crowd, no one was going to notice a group of dirty, limping pirates, scribes, mermaids, and traitors.

Siddhe had dumped him unceremoniously on his bed and rushed to get the ship on its way, as far away from Withrae as fast as possible. Gavin had sustained some injury to his shoulder and had been taken below deck with the girl. She'd have to care for him because no one else would have the time to spare while they were trying to get away. He hoped to hell that she could keep him alive.

The last thing he wanted to do was to have to find another scribe while trying to figure out just how his quest involved this prince-murdering, gallows-escaping, half-blood dragon girl.

Why could nothing ever be easy?

CHAPTER SIXTEEN

THE SHIP AWAITED JUST ON the choppy water as rain fell in thick sheets from the sky. Rowen had just escaped death, and still wasn't entirely convinced that she wasn't dreaming.

"Hey, we're almost there, sir," Rowen said.

"Gavin," he said. "Call me Gavin."

Gavin fought to catch his breath and Rowen helped him board. The adrenaline that pumped through her veins kept her from passing out on the slick wooden floor.

Elian shouted above the noise of the port to set sail. Rowen and Gavin sat on the floor near the ship's railing. She looked up at him, her chest heaving. She'd seen that face before.

Several times.

That man—the stranger from her dreams—had saved her life. And, the way he had done it was nothing short of spectacular.

A sorcerer. If only she had a shred of his power, she'd never be anyone's prisoner ever again.

As if he read her thoughts, his gray eyes lowered to hers. The moment was brief, but she could feel something spark between them like a forgotten memory or a promise of revelations to come. She swallowed and turned her attention to the young man at her side.

He winced when she touched his bloodied shirt.

"Are you all right?"

"Just a few broken ribs," Gavin said with a shrug. "I'll live."

Rowen sucked her teeth and narrowed her eyes as she pulled his shirt up for a better look. An arrow protruded from his shoulder.

"Oh, and I've been shot," he added. "Brilliant."

"Do you have supplies on the ship? Any stringent or bandages?"

"Wish I knew. I've only been on this ship for a few days."

Siddhe walked by, her boots thumping on the deck, splashing water with each step.

"Ma'am," Rowen called.

Siddhe stopped and turned to her, a cold look in her ethereal eyes. "What?"

The question was forceful and much louder than Rowen expected. It didn't take much for her to realize that that woman did not like her.

Nonetheless, she had to help Gavin. No one else seemed to care that he was bleeding on deck and in more pain than he let on.

She nodded to Gavin's injuries. "Is there somewhere I can take him to tend to his wounds?"

Siddhe pointed to the stairs that led below deck. "Down there," she shouted. "Now, stay out of my way."

There was no mistaking the malice in the woman's voice. She would indeed stay out of her way. Rowen frowned as Siddhe stomped away to join the crew in setting sail. She peered over the railing as the ship rocked and swayed and pulled away from the docks. The protesters were rioting and yelling after the ship. Still, they weren't jumping into the water or boarding ships to come after her.

For now, they were safe.

It would be hours before Withrae's navy could organize a search party for her. She just hoped the ship she was swept away on was fast enough to outrun them. Then again, she knew nothing about the people who kidnapped her. What would they want with a convicted prince killer?

She didn't know. But, she had to help the young man that helped her escape her execution.

"Don't mind her," Gavin said, breaking her from her thoughts. "Siddhe hates everyone. 'Cept the captain."

Sighing, Rowen came to her feet and helped Gavin up. "I'm not worried about her. I just want to make sure you don't bleed to death."

"Why, is that kind of you?" Gavin said with a forced smirk.

She lowered his arm over her shoulder and led him to the stairs, careful not to get in the way of the men that stood on deck.

Some raced to their stations, others watched her with great interest.

Once they were down the stairs and below deck, Gavin nodded to a cabin at the far end of the dimly lit hallway. "There, that's where they keep the weapons and the supplies."

"Gavin," Rowen called as she helped him stumble to the door, and pushed it open.

"What?"

Rowen closed the door behind him. She settled him into a wooden chair and knelt before him, her eyes boring into his.

"Am I safe here?"

He stared back at her for a moment. The color of his cheeks had already drained to a color much paler than when they'd first met.

"Am I?" Rowen asked again.

Gavin took her hand into his and closed his fingers around it. He nodded, taking in a sigh. "Yes. You are safe. We didn't save you to harm you, miss."

Relieved, Rowen closed her eyes and exhaled. "Okay. Good. I just had to know."

"No worries. I'd be a bit wary of being on a ship full of pirates too."

Rowen's eyes popped open. Her cheeks paled. "Pirates?"

Gavin cracked a surprised grin. He coughed out a laugh. "What did you think this was? A traveling side show?"

Rowen groaned.

Gavin pulled her close until her face was only inches from his. "Hey," he said. "It's fine. I told you that you were safe. You have to trust me."

Rowen licked her lips, uncomfortable with how close they were. He was a stranger.

A handsome one... but a stranger no less.

"Trust you?"

He nodded and winced again. "Yes. Trust me, and get this arrow out of my blasted arm."

"Oh," Rowen said, remembering how much pain he was in. She stood up and held onto one end of the arrow. "How do I do this?" She looked at the sharp end and the blunt end. She couldn't just slide it out without further damage to his flesh.

"Break the sharp end and pull it out."

Rowen rubbed her hands together and nodded, giving herself courage. "Okay."

She took one end, and with all of her strength, pushed the tip down, breaking it off.

"Good girl," Gavin said.

Then, she pulled the arrow free and blood came gushing from his wound. Gavin let out a cry of pain and a squeal escaped Rowen's lips and she hurried to pull his shirt over his head and used it to press into the wound.

"Don't worry," she said. "Everything is fine." She said the words to reassure herself more than anything.

"I ain't no warrior. I told Captain Elian such. But, no. He insists that I have to save the girl."

Rowen shook her head. "I don't know how you all did it. But, I am grateful."

She found a crate full of bandages and casks of water. She opened the cask and removed his bloody shirt. Pouring the water on the wound cleaned off the blood and dirt. She ripped the bandage and wrapped it tightly around Gavin's shoulder. And another around his black and blue ribs.

"Were you a healer?" Gavin asked, and she noticed how intently he watched her.

Rowen shook her head. "I wish," she whispered. "No. I was a lady-in-waiting to the princess of Withrae."

"Dangerous job, aye?"

Rowen tilted her head and let out a laugh. "You have no idea."

She paused when he lifted his hand and traced the bruise where the noose had been. Her body stiffened and she closed her eyes against the memories of facing her death. She'd faced it many times in her dreams. But, that morning had been the first time it had felt utterly real. She backed away, her eyes still closed, and sucked up her tears.

"Hey," Gavin said, softly.

Rowen opened her eyes. His voice was soothing, and his eyes were innocent. Out of everyone on that ship, she felt that she could trust him.

"Yes?"

"You're safe now," he said.

Sliding to the ground, Rowen settled against the door and finally let down her guard. The moment she did, she realized just how exhausted she was.

"I could sleep for days," she said.

"Let me take you to a cabin." Gavin tried to push himself up to his feet, but Rowen crawled over and placed a hand on his other shoulder.

"No. Stay put. I'm in no rush."

He placed a hand on hers. "It's no problem. I'll get you settled."

Rowen bit the corner of her lip, her brows furrowing. "I'm afraid to be alone on this ship."

He searched her eyes and then sighed. She watched him ponder for a moment, before taking her hand and helping her to her feet. With a little effort and a grimace, he stood and led her back to the door.

"Let me at least get you to a cabin where you can get comfortable."

Before Rowen could protest, Gavin shushed her by putting a finger to his lips.

"I'll stay with you. You know, guard you while you sleep."

She stood on the back of her heels, a bit taken aback by his offer.

Without hesitation, she nodded. Anything was better than being alone on a pirate ship full of strangers. Even if Gavin was technically as much as a stranger as the rest, she just helped him avoid bleeding out. He owed her that much.

"Right," he said, and opened the door. "Off we go."

CHAPTER SEVENTEEN

RELIEF WASHED OVER ROWEN AS she followed Gavin down the narrow hallway to a turn to the right.

"Right this way. Watch your step. Some of the floorboards are a bit... delicate."

The ships wooden walls were cracked in some places and worn in others. She'd never been on a ship before and with each creak of the floorboards and the constant swaying that nearly knocked her from her feet, she wondered if it was indeed seaworthy.

She hated to be rescued from the gallows only to drown.

He stopped before a door and turned the knob, opening it for her.

"I could have done that," Rowen said, worried about his arm.

"Hey," he said. "I'm not too weak to open a door, miss."

Before she went inside, she looked behind her to the cabin right across from hers.

"Is that the captain's room?" Rowen asked as she took a step closer for a better look. The cabin was much larger than the one Gavin claimed was her own. There was a large wooden desk covered with maps and rolled scrolls. In the corner, she saw a claw foot tub and in the other corner sat a bed with a canopy.

"That's right. You're on a boat full of pirates. Some of them haven't seen a woman in over a year from what I've heard. 'Cept for Siddhe. She's a mermaid and belongs to the captain."

"Oh," Rowen said, her brows lifting. She knew there was something different about the woman.

"I hate to speak ill of any of them, since I don't know anyone here very well... but I'm going to anyway. You want to be where you're going to stay safe from," he coughed and gave her a pointed look that struck home. "Male attention... if you get my meaning, miss."

She did get his meaning and a wave of nausea washed over her. If all she had was a wounded human and a pirate captain that looked at her with disdain to protect her from the other men, she was going to need to figure out a better way to look out for herself.

"Yes," she whispered, turning away from the captain's room. She glanced at Gavin. "I get it." She nodded and stepped inside, her hands folded before her. A quick look around the room and she settled on the short bed that was pushed against the wall. There was a single crate, an oil lamp, and a chest for storing things.

Gavin sat on the chest and turned his body so that his back was pressed to the wall and his legs were long ways over the rest of the chest.

The rocking of the ship was unnerving, as was the crashing of thunder she heard outside.

"It's storming?"

Gavin looked up to the ceiling, listening. "Sounds like it."

She avoided staring at his bare chest. Her mother would die if she knew Rowen was alone with a half-dressed man in a bedroom.

Rowen shook her head. What did it matter? Her former life was over, and so were the trivial ideals she'd been brought up with. Her reputation was already destroyed. There was no coming back from being deemed a murderer. To add to it, the entire kingdom would know that she was a magic user as well.

Nevertheless, she was alive. Every minute that she was free from the noose was a minute longer than her prophecy foretold. Life. That was all Rowen cared about. She may have a bruise where the noose had been, but breath still filled her lungs. Whatever happened from here on out would build her new history.

Until the next prophecy presented itself.

She did something she hadn't done since she was a little girl. She chewed her thumb's nail and pondered how she changed the prophecy. Only a prophet could do such a thing, and she searched her memory for an instant where she'd altered things.

Gavin coughed and she stood to take a look at his bandages. A spot of blood had already seeped through the thick cloth.

She frowned as she made sure his bandages were tight enough. "I'll have to change those in a few hours," she told him.

"Whatever you say. I'm in your hands."

Rowen ran her fingertips along his shoulder.

"You're human? Aren't you?"

Gavin gave her a sidelong glance. "What of it?"

She tore her eyes away from his half-naked body and shook her head. "You've no scales, is all. I've never met a human man before."

He lifted a brow. "I've never seen a half-blood Dragon before either. Where are your scales? Can you fly?"

The ship rocked forcefully and Rowen fell onto Gavin's chest. She held onto his neck as she steadied herself. He wrapped an arm around her and held her as the ship seemed to teeter on its side.

"Good gracious," she said, squeezing her eyes shut. She couldn't drown. Not after everything she'd been through. But, the fear of being trapped in a sinking ship gripped her and wouldn't let go.

The ship rocked back and seemed to settle.

Rowen looked up to Gavin with widened eyes. She didn't let go until she was certain that everything was safe.

"Don't worry, miss. Just a feisty wave is all."

Rowen realized how tightly she held onto Gavin, and how close his face was to hers. She let go and hurried back to her bed. Rowen pulled her feet up. It squeaked as she did so.

"Not used to the sea, are you?"

"No," Rowen said, a bit embarrassed by her show of terror.

"It's all right. Most women aren't used to it. I'm only just getting my sea legs. I'm a land kind of bloke. But, I'm learning to like it."

"I just hope we find land and I'm allowed to go free."

"Ah, don't worry about that. You are free."

"Am I?"

Gavin shrugged. "No one told me otherwise. Say, you didn't answer me. Where are your scales, and can you fly?"

Rowen shook her head and started to calm down as the ship continued to speed across the sea. At least it didn't tilt again.

"I'm only half Dragon. We don't have enough Dragon blood to change and fly."

"Oh. None of that matters on the Wandering Star."

"Is that the name of the ship?"

"That's right," Gavin said. "She may be old, but she's fast and strong."

Thunder rumbled from above, vibrating the entire cabin. Rowen held onto her arms. "I definitely hope so," she mumbled.

"Don't worry your pretty little head. Captain Elian will never let this ship go down. It's his baby."

"I'm sorry, but my life is on the line. I'm going to worry."

"Suit yourself."

"What can you tell me about the captain?"

Gavin shrugged, and for the first time Rowen felt him grow cold to her. "Not much to tell. I'm only his scribe."

"But, who is he? What kind of man is he?"

"I wish I could help you there, miss. He's been decent to me so far. But, remember, I've only been here less than a week. I don't know much more than you."

Rowen nodded. He wasn't going to tell anything.

That was frightening. She couldn't help but worry about what he was hiding. She glanced at the door and noticed that there wasn't a lock.

As if sensing the change in mood, Gavin stood. "I'm going on deck to see how things are going. I can bring you some food if you're hungry."

Rowen shook her head. "I'm going to get some rest," she said, despite the fact that her stomach growled and churned with hunger.

Gavin lingered in the doorway. For a moment, Rowen thought there was something he wanted to say, and she watched him, hopeful.

Instead, he gave a nod and opened the door. "Get settled and I'll come and check on you later. Sleep well, miss. If you can."

Before he left, Rowen considered using her power on him and forcing the information out. Unease filled her belly. But, she couldn't bring herself to do it, and simply watched him leave and close the door behind him.

Once she was alone, Rowen hugged her legs to her chest and tried to control her breathing. The anxiety from being kidnapped by pirates flooded her all at once.

Not knowing what plans they had for her made her skin tighten with dread.

Did they plan to sell her? Would she end up a slave or servant in a faraway land to a cruel master, or kept on the ship to pleasure the crew?

Neither concept was comforting. All she was left with was Gavin's reassurance that she was safe, and that her cabin was right across from the captains'.

She just wished she knew who that man was, and why he had haunted her dreams.

CHAPTER EIGHTEEN

ROWEN WAS AWAKENED BY HEAVY footsteps entering her cabin. She sat up with a start and scrambled up to her elbows. Was it morning? She felt as though she'd slept for ages but had no way of knowing the hour.

Groggily, she beheld Siddhe standing at the foot of her bed. The tall woman put her hands on her curvy hips and peered down at her.

"Get up," she said. "Come with me."

Shaking off sleep, she came to her feet. She was tired, sore, and her stomach screamed for sustenance. She hesitated to follow the woman who clearly disliked her.

"Where are we going?" Rowen dared to ask.

Siddhe scoffed. "You're better off keeping your questions to yourself."

Before Rowen could reply, Siddhe stepped outside of her room and headed across the hall.

"Come on, girl. I don't have all day to wait for you." The look in Siddhe's eyes told her that she dared not even think about saying another word.

Rowen left the small measure of safety she felt from her cabin. At least the storm seemed to have abated, and the ship sailed without bumps and dips.

Siddhe knocked on the captain's door and turned to stare down at her. Rowen averted her eyes. There was something odd about Siddhe's eyes, something that was unsettling, as if the woman not only disliked her, but could read what was written on her soul.

"Come in," a muffled voice said from the other side of the door.

Siddhe turned the knob and pushed the door open. She looked to Rowen and nodded for her to go inside.

Reluctant, Rowen first peered inside. She could feel the heat coming from the brazier, and the scent of burning candles affronted her nostrils.

Inside, it was cozy. Cozier than her tiny cabin. And, as her stomach grumbled, there was food.

Breakfast.

The sight of Hard cheese, dried meat, dried fruit, and ale on the table ushered her feet forward. Siddhe no longer existed. Only her desire to calm the turmoil in her belly.

"Join me," Captain Elian said. "You can go."

Rowen glanced back to see Siddhe roll her eyes and slammed the door.

"Come," he said. "Sit."

His cabin was comfortable, home-like. Maps covered every inch of this walls, some in languages she'd never seen. Others of places she never knew existed.

He nodded to a chair across from him and she lowered herself onto it. It took everything within her to restrain herself from grabbing food from the platters and stuffing her face. She couldn't remember the last meal she'd had. Bread and water were not enough to sate anyone's hunger, and that was all she was allowed in Withrae Prison.

She frowned as she looked at the food, terribly upset by what she'd been reduced to. She looked to Elian, as if waiting for permission to partake of his meal.

Elian seemed to notice her dilemma, and she wiped tears from her eyes.

"I'm guessing you haven't eaten in days," he said, taking a bit of cheese and watching her with curious eyes.

Rowen shook her head, biting the corner of her bottom lip.

"Well, go on," he said with a nod. "Eat up.

She didn't need to be told twice. She took a chunk of cheese and pressed it against the hard bread. The first bite was euphoric. It wasn't anything like what she had back at home or in the palace, but the crunch of the bread and the tangy spice of the cheese brought a satisfied smile to her face as she closed her eyes and relished the flavor.

Elian didn't exist for a few moments as Rowen worked to calm her hunger. She ripped through the tough meat with her teeth and chewed it until softened. She drank her entire mug of mild ale without stopping for a breath.

This was not lady-like.

Rowen did not care.

She kept her eyes closed as she chewed her food and felt her belly start to fill. Then, she opened them to find Elian watching her, his chin resting on his fist.

"What is it?"

He shrugged. "Curious, is all. Tell me, who are you?"

Rowen held out her mug, and he poured her more ale.

She drank a few sips and wiped her mouth. "Who are you?"

His eye twitched. "I asked first, young lady. Don't forget that I am the one who saved your life. You'd be half-way to the spirt world by now if I hadn't come along."

Rowen nodded. "True. But, I'm not going to reveal myself without knowing who you are and what you want."

"Like I said, I saved your life. Tell me."

"Not if you're going to kill me because of who I turn out to be or who you turn out to be."

In his eyes, she saw the same raw, steely wile she harbored, except his was tempered and razor sharp, and it honestly frightened her.

She held his glare a bit before she realized that he wasn't going to budge.

Shoulders slumping, Rowen gave in. "I'm Lady Rowen Glenick of Harrow. My mother is Duchess Nimah Glenick and my stepfather is the Duke of Harrow, Brecks Glenick. My real father is dead." She sighed and continued. "I was a lady-in-waiting for Princess Noemie of Withrae when I was accused of the crown prince's murder. I'm innocent. But, that doesn't matter when they need someone to blame."

Rowen paused. Elian's face had morphed from quiet calculation to disbelief and confusion.

"What? Did I say something wrong?"

He became withdrawn, as if lost in his own thoughts. He shook his head and returned to his meal. The silence that followed was uncomfortable. The level of tension in the room had risen to a level that heated Rowen's cheeks.

Rowen wasn't sure of what to do. Stay? Leave? She guessed that her reply was suitable and took a bit of cheese. "It's your turn, Captain. What are you going to do with me?"

Noncommittally, he shrugged and avoided her widened eyes.

"Siddhe," he called, and the woman burst into the room. She'd clearly been outside the entire time, listening.

Rowen took another bite of cheese, not ready to end her meal.

Elian looked to Siddhe. "Take her back to her cabin. Have Gavin stay with her."

Rowen's jaw dropped as Siddhe lifted her from her chair by her arms.

She shot a glare at the woman. "Get your hands off of me," she hissed.

Siddhe grinned and held her hands up. "Sorry, miss," she taunted.

Annoyed, Rowen glanced at Elian one more time to see that he had stood from the table and had his back turned to her. He rubbed his chin and stared at his map, no longer interested in her in the least.

With a huff, Rowen left the cabin and folded her arms across her chest. Gavin came down the stairs and joined them outside of the captain's cabin.

"Stay with the girl," Siddhe ordered. "Captain wants to make sure she stays out of trouble. Understood?"

Gavin shrugged. "Shouldn't be hard," he said, giving the frustrated Rowen a smile. "She's a good girl. I can vouch for her."

Siddhe scoffed. "Good girl my arse," she said, and pushed past them both to return to the upper deck.

Rowen frowned. What had just happened? She gave up her identity and learned nothing in return. Why did he become so spooked when she revealed it to him?

Sighing, she went back into her cabin and Gavin followed. Once he settled back on the chest, Rowen shut the door and turned to him.

It was time to get some answers, and she was willing to use her power to do it.

CHAPTER NINETEEN

THE HOURS ROLLED BY AS Rowen worked her charms on Gavin. She would do what she could and obtain as much information as possible before resorting to using magic.

He was a handsome man, and it wasn't difficult to like him and test her flirtation on him. Still, she wasn't there for romance. Her life was still on the line, and that's all Rowen had ever cared about.

Survival.

"How was your breakfast with the captain?" Gavin asked.

"Unexpected," Rowen replied as she pulled his bandage off. She narrowed her eyes as she examined his wound. It hadn't healed much, but the bleeding had slowed. "This doesn't look bad. Not bad at all."

"Maybe you should have been a healer," Gavin said, as he watched her. "You're quite good at it."

Rowen smiled and shrugged. "I suppose. I'm good at a great many things, but none of that matters now." She placed the bloody bandage on the empty crate and pulled a fresh one from the basket of supplies she had him bring to her.

"Maybe it does," Gavin said. "Now that you can start a new life. You can use what skills you have. Just a thought."

Rowen glanced at him. He was right, if only she knew that she would be free to live her own life. That would be a dream come true.

"Maybe," she muttered.

"So, what do you think of the captain now that you've had a meal with him?"

Rowen's mouth twisted as she thought. "He certainly has the mysterious thing down. I honestly know less about him that I did before. He's vexing."

"To say the least," Gavin added and they shared a laugh.

"I just have the feeling that he knows more about me than he lets on. I just want the same in return. I asked him what he was going to do with me... and he shrugged it off without a reply. How long am I supposed to live in fear?"

Gavin steadied her hand, and covered it with his own. Rowen's brows bunched as she realized that her hands were shaking.

"Hey," he said, softly. "You have nothing to fear. You hear me?"

Rowen flickered a look at his face. His eyes were a soft brown, and without a trace of dishonesty. She wanted to believe him.

She nodded, and he yawned. "Almost finished?"

Rowen wrapped the new bandage around his arrow wound and clasped her hands before her, taking a step back to check out her handiwork. "I believe so."

"Good," he said, and settled his head against the wall. "I need a nap, if you don't mind?"

Rowen sat on her bed and watched him close his eyes. She wanted to press him for more answers, but it seemed that he was being kept in the dark as much as she was. He didn't know anything of value.

Gavin yawned again. "Wake me up when Logan delivers dinner."

Rowen's brows rose. "So, we are supposed to stay in here all day? And you insist I am not a prisoner."

He winked at her. "Keeping you safe, remember?"

Rowen pursed her lips and shook her head as Gavin drifted to sleep. She watched him for a while, noting how peaceful he looked with his eyes closed and snoring softly. She should have offered him her bed. The chest didn't look the least bit comfortable.

She realized that she'd never seen Prince Lawson sleep, or much more than their stolen secreted moments together in various parts of the palace. Her heart was still broken. It had only been a week since she lost him, and his image continued to pop up when she was left in solitude. Finding his killer wasn't an option anymore. She would never return to Withrae or the land of her birth. Now that she was with pirates, she wondered if her destiny awaited in the human realm.

Such a prospect was terrifying. She'd never dreamed of going to the human kingdoms, but now that it was actually an option it frightened her. She was on her own, for the first time in her life.

She glanced at Gavin and twirled a lock of her hair around her finger. She just had to get away from the pirates.

Yawning, Rowen settled onto her hard bed and closed her eyes. Just a few winks of sleep would give her the energy she needed to continue working her charms on Gavin. Before she could fall asleep, a prophecy flooded her mind, and pinned her down to her bed so that she couldn't move. She could barely breathe as the scent of blood and burnt coal filled her nostrils.

When Rowen opened her eyes, she was taken aback by the amount of bodies that littered the red dirt of a mountain valley. She covered her mouth, overwhelmed by the smell and sight of death and carnage.

Gavin's dead body was at her feet, his cold lifeless eyes directed to the sky which was a blend of red, purple and orange.

"Dear fire and light," she whispered as she looked over the cliff at a sea of blood.

When she spun around, the sight was the same.

Death.

Everywhere.

Captain Elian's body hung from a tall, black tree just feet behind her with a sign that said "sorcerer" scratched into it with blood. Siddhe was dead at the base, impaled by her own sword.

Why Rowen was alive was a mystery.

"Did I do this?"

Rowen prayed that it wasn't so. She may have been an accused and convicted murderer, but she'd never killed anyone and never dreamed of such.

A loud screech startled her, and as Rowen turned back to the cliff, a red dragon flew to her, it's beautiful wings spanning no more than a large bird's.

Instinctively, Rowen outstretched her left arm, and sucked in a breath of surprise as the red dragon landed on it, just above her wrist.

It turned a golden eye to meet hers and bowed.

It spoke. "Where shall we go now?"

Rowen shot to her elbows, disoriented and fuzzy-headed. It took a moment to even see straight, let alone for the thumping in her head to subside.

Once the prophecy faded, Rowen's dress clung to her skin with sweat. She'd never had one so confusing before. It left her feeling uneasy and exposed.

Rowen slid off the bed and onto her feet. Quietly, she peeked over at Gavin's face to see that he was sleeping soundly. Seeing him dead in her prophecy made her stomach churn. She barely knew him, but she didn't want to see him meet that awful fate.

Satisfied that he wouldn't be going anywhere for a while, she straightened her dress and quickly braided her hair into a single braid that hung down her back.

Perhaps it was time to investigate on her own. Now that she was armed with a new prophecy, she needed to stay one step ahead of it. At least in this new one she was alive.

She flinched when a soft knock came from the door. Rowen quickly answered, hoping to prevent another from waking Gavin. An older crewman stood outside the door, wearing a dingy brown apron over his leather pants and tucked in shirt. He had sunken blue eyes and stringy grayish-brown hair that fell into his eyes.

"Logan, is it?"

He nodded and she looked down to the plates of cheese, beans, and bread he had in his hand.

"Dinner, miss," he said as she accepted the food.

Rowen set the plates on the empty crate and before Logan could get away, she rushed back to him and took his hand into her own.

He tensed, and then went limp at her touch.

"Stay with Gavin, won't you?" She asked with a sweet smile.

Logan's eyes widened and he nodded. "Of course, miss. I'll stay with Gavin."

"Good," Rowen said, patting his roughened hand. "Sit there, and watch him for me."

Dutifully, Logan sat on the bed and turned his gaze to the sleeping young scribe.

Pleased with the effectiveness of her bewitching of the old pirate, Rowen walked over to Gavin, placed a hand on his forehead, and leaned close to his ear.

"Stay asleep until I return to wake you," she whispered and his head lolled to the left, toward the wall.

Rowen grinned as she stood. She rubbed her hands together. "Good," she said. "Now, let's get some answers."

She left the safety of her cabin and peered around both corners from the doorway. No one was coming.

She jumped and retreated to her room, closing the door quietly as she heard footsteps coming down the hallway.

Siddhe's footsteps. Already she knew them well, the click of her boots, and the rustling of the keys at her belt.

She listened as Siddhe walked right into Captain Elian's office without bothering to knock.

Once the door opened and closed, Rowen carefully opened her door and stepped out into the hallway.

Her heart thumped in her chest. This would be dangerous. But, she had no other choice. Sitting around and waiting to be sold or killed was out of the question. She'd bewitch them all if she had to.

Rowen pressed her cheek to Elian's door, and listened.

CHAPTER TWENTY

SO, THAT WAS NIMAH'S DAUGHTER?

He rolled the name Nimah Glenick around on his tongue and found it tasted sour. Nimah Vasour had sounded... and tasted so much sweeter.

But apparently, she had turned out to be an ambitious little bitch, just like her mother and father. Married a duke. Served her purpose as a right little brood mare, producing a chit just in her likeness.

And, just as ruthless, if the charge of murdering the crown prince of Withrae was to be believed.

Elian jumped to his feet and flipped the table over with a cry of frustration. Pewter and porcelain went crashing, and ale slinked into the cracks of the wood floor.

All that power expended, all those dark souls lost, all for the sake of what, saving Nimah's brat? What the bloody hell did that have to do with the Red Dragon? The Vasours were Mount Withrae Dragons with ice in their blood, and in their hearts. Every last one of them.

There was nothing special among the nobility of Draconia. Every dragon family claimed some mountain or other, and what did that make them? A bunch of overgrown lizards crowing over owning a piece of rock.

He wondered with a wry smile what they would have done about their magnificent lineages if Draconia had been all desert. They would have had to play king of the sand dune, only to have it all blow away.

All the same, Rowen Glenick's presence made him think twice about dismissing Withrae as being significant in the quest for the Red Dragon. It was a damn shame that he had just complicated getting back into the kingdom by foiling the execution of its most wanted criminal.

Pacing around the cabin, despite the residual exhaustion from expending all the dark souls, he replayed Cota's words. Nothing fit when it came to Rowen.

She wasn't his heart's desire. She wasn't any kind of desire for him. For one thing, she was far too young, and for another, he felt slightly sick at the idea of bedding Nimah's daughter. If nothing else, Siddhe would have his balls if he looked at the girl wrong, and he liked his balls right where they were. Siddhe did, too.

As if he had conjured her, the mermaid strode into his cabin without bothering to knock. She glanced without emotion at the overturned table and spilled food.

"Storm's passed." One look at Siddhe showed that while the weather may have cleared, her own personal storm was brewing and just about to break loose.

"Where'd we end up?" He hadn't set any particular orders before they left, just to get them out of there.

"In the middle of the ocean." She shrugged.

Elian managed a weak snort at that.

"Correction," she added. "In the middle of the ocean, waiting like sitting ducks for the Withraen navy."

"It could have been any ship that took the girl. We weren't the only ones buggering out of port that day."

"I give that scribe boy's barmaid exactly two minutes under a stern glare before she tells the royal inquisitors everything."

"Well, as you said, we're in the middle of the ocean. We didn't even know where we were sailing to, so how could they?"

Siddhe looked ready to slap him upside the head.

"The girl is from Harrow," she spat.

She didn't need to say anything more. He knew what she meant. If Rowen was part of the mystery and came from Harrow, then the next logical step was to go back to Harrow.

"Torture her." Siddhe's voice was even but deadly cold.

Elian considered it. "Why?"

"She must know something, even if she doesn't know it. Pain begets answers."

The memory of his vision of Rowen falling with the noose around her neck pulsed behind his eyes. He hadn't had a prophesy in so long. Decades. That's why he had needed Cota. The vision of Rowen had to mean something.

"She might talk of her own accord," Elian mused. "Without torture."

Siddhe's incredulous expression came uncomfortably close to the way he looked at Gavin.

"The right questions may get answers she doesn't know she has," he pointed out.

"Then, take your time with her, by all means. Might as well let the Withraen navy catch up."

"There are times, Siddhe, when you begin to sound alarmingly like me."

"There are times when you are a fool."

Elian huffed in amusement and walked over to his desk. He leaned over, bracing his hands against the surface. He pressed his lips together in an effort to ignore the faint discomfort coming from the very center of his bones. Concentrating on the large parchment before him helped somewhat.

The parchment was old, with age browning and shredding the edges and corners. Read from left-to-right, it was obviously a map, but it looked only half-finished. Elian focused his anger on the blank half of the map. It was there. All those drawings that would lead him to the Red Dragon were there. Just hidden.

Every landmark on the map so far had been bought with blood and peril. The first few had been the angry buccaneering of a young man with a broken heart. The second handful were the object of a man whose life was empty of everything else but a pointless purpose. The hidden marks in the blank space mocked him, now when his very life depended on succeeding in this quest.

He couldn't afford to dismiss any clue, even if it came in the form of a silly little girl who had been the catspaw in an undoubtedly bigger political game.

"We head for Harrow, then?" Siddhe's voice called him back from his thoughts.

He nodded once, wearily.

There was a loud crash behind him, and he winced, not really wanting to know what Siddhe had smashed.

"When will you stop?" she demanded. There was a breathless, desperate edge to her voice. "Your endless dreaming of someday will make you lose all that you have today!"

He moved to Siddhe and wrapped her in his arms. "Dreaming of someday is all that makes this day bearable. That, and you, my lovely little sea monster."

Siddhe's kisses were full of salt, either from her ocean blood or her tears.

If only they could have been enough to reconcile a dying man to his fate.

TORTURE?

Shaking, Rowen pulled away from the door. She'd heard enough. She'd escaped torture and death. Now, these pirates wanted to treat her like a prisoner again. Could she never truly win?

She retreated to her cabin before Siddhe and the captain finished having sex with one another. Her heart raced, and yet she had no outlet for the fear that gripped at her.

Logan sat on her bed like a statue, his eyes on Gavin as if his life depended on it.

She placed a hand on his cheek. "You should get back to the kitchen. Don't you think?" She tried to keep her voice light and sweet as her mind fought to think of a way to get off that ship.

Logan nodded. "Right, miss. I'm s'pposed to be feedin' the crew."

"Good man," she said, and watched him leave the room.

She knelt before Gavin and whispered into his ear, while holding his hand. "You're free to wake up whenever you'd like."

Gavin's body relaxed and with a sigh, Rowen pushed herself back up to her feet.

She stood in the center of the room, staring at the closed cabin door. So many questions. Still, very little answers.

Why would they need to torture her for answers? She was certain that she didn't know anything useful to them.

CHAPTER TWENTY-ONE

THREE BRUTAL DAYS OF WAITING had passed and Rowen was still unsure of her place on the ship. She lived in fear, and utter boredom, with only Gavin to comfort and entertain her. When they moved her from her cabin to another darker, muskier, smaller cabin on another level, her confusion only grew. The bed was the only piece of furniture in her new cabin, and she was forced to eat her meals off of her lap like a stable hand rushing in between shoveling dung.

Gavin—her protector—had returned to his duties on the ship and only came to her when they were done. His wounds were healing, but he was still weakened.

Twice, Elian called for Rowen and questioned her. Each time was more frustrating than the last.

On the second day, Captain Elian summoned her again. This time he had questions about her Dragon abilities. With a straight face, Rowen told him that she had none.

"Silly, useless girl," he called her, but her answer satisfied him and he allowed her to go.

On the third day, he called for her. Questions about Prince Lawson and whether she killed him were addressed. Vehemently, Rowen swore that she had loved Lawson and had been framed for his murder.

Again, Captain Elian believed her. This time it was the truth. Either the captain truly took her for her word, or was only pretending to. The latter frightened her. There was a quiet mystery about that man that she couldn't shake. The way his ice-gray eyes lingered on her face and examined her always left her unsettled for hours after their meetings ended.

All Rowen wanted was fresh air, a good hot meal, a warm comfortable bed, and her freedom.

When Gavin visited her that evening, Rowen didn't waste any time. She stood from her small, rickety bed, which took up most of the room.

"Gavin," she said, wringing her hands. "You have to tell me what they have planned. Don't let me sit here awaiting my death? Not again. Please."

He held his hands out and clicked his teeth. "Now, who told you that you were going to die? Didn't I say that you were safe? Come now, you're supposed to trust me."

"Why are we going to Harrow?"

Gavin tensed. He hid his surprise, but it was too late. Now, she knew he was hiding things. In just hours they would be docking in her hometown. The concept was both terrifying and exciting. If only she knew why.

"Where did you hear that?"

Rowen placed her hands on her hips. "Logan," she said. "Seems he tells me more than you do. And, I'm supposed to trust you?"

She turned away from him, feigning indignation. Her cheeks were flushed, and her breathing had quickened. She pulled her dress away from her chest, letting in more air. That cabin was hot and stuffy, and she was sick of being there. Why they moved her in the first place was a mystery.

"Rowen," Gavin called.

"No," she said. "You don't care if I live or die. Just admit it." Her words were petulant, but would appeal to his softer side. She needed him to let down his guard and see her for the poor, defenseless young lady that she was. That was the angle she chose to play this time.

Anything to get him to tell her the truth.

When he took her by the arm, Rowen softened against his touch. Gently, he turned her to face him.

For a moment, she felt as if she looked at Lawson. The way Gavin tilted her chin with his fingers almost brought her to tears. Instead of crying, she looked into his eyes, pleadingly.

"What's the worst that can happen if you just tell me what's going on?"

Gavin shook his head. "I can end up dead is all." His eyes locked on her lips. When he licked his own, Rowen had the urge to just take him by the face and kiss him. It was stronger than she'd expected, and difficult to fight. She was sure that his lips tasted as delicious as they looked.

Rowen did take him by the face, with both hands, and lowered her voice to a dangerous snarl.

"Tell me what you know about Captain Elian's plans for me. Why are we going to Harrow?"

His words about dying nagged at her. She didn't want him to die for revealing secrets, but no one would have to know.

Gavin grabbed her hand, his brows furrowing, and he smacked her hand back. "What do you think you're doing?"

Mortified, Rowen's jaw hung. Did it not work?

"Did you... just try to bewitch me?"

"Gavin, listen. I didn't mean it."

"Bloody hell," he said, and Rowen realized that she'd wounded him. Not physically, but emotionally.

Maybe he trusted her more than she trusted him.

Gavin took a step away from her and rubbed his cheeks. Without removing his gaze, he left her room and shook his head.

Alone once more, Rowen fell to the floor.

It didn't work.

She covered her mouth. How could she be so foolish? She thought back to the only time she had attempted her power of persuasion on Gavin.

He'd been asleep.

"Stupid, foolish girl," she mumbled. Nothing would calm the pain in her belly. Nothing would erase the fact that now the captain would know that she lied about not having any abilities.

Rowen's head hung. "Just my luck."

CHAPTER TWENTY-TWO

LUNCH ARRIVED, AND ROWEN WAS tired of waiting. If Gavin was going to go and tell on her, she wanted to be there to defend and explain herself.

Instead of accepting the plate of the same old bread and cheese, she moved it aside and gave him a firm look.

"Take me Captain Elian," she ordered.

Logan scratched his hair. "I don't know about that, miss. Captain would surely have my hide. You're supposed to stay in your cabin. Everyone knows that."

Rowen took him by the hand. Her power surged from her palm and into his, silencing his protests.

Again, she spoke. This time, through clenched teeth. "Take me to the captain."

"Yes, ma'am," Logan said. "This way."

The fact that she couldn't use her power on Gavin left her more vulnerable than she was before. She had no way of knowing if it would work on the captain or Siddhe if she needed to protect herself. But, the waiting and uncertainty was almost as bad as nearly freezing to death in Withrae Prison.

The narrow hallway was stifling, and the sound of shouting pirates above did little to erase her fears. The farther they walked, the more Rowen started to wonder if the captain intentionally wanted her as far from him as possible. She followed Logan up a few stairs and to another level of the ship.

When they arrived, Logan lingered, watching Rowen as if waiting for another order.

Sighing, she gently placed her hand to his cheek. "Go back to work."

He nodded. "Right. Back to work."

Rowen bottled her fear, took a deep breath, and knocked on the door.

Instead of a voice coming from the other side, the door opened almost immediately.

Rowen gulped.

There stood Siddhe, the same look of disdain and distrust on her beautiful face.

She grabbed Rowen by the front of her dress. "What are you doing here?"

Glancing around her, Rowen looked to Captain Elian who sat at his desk. Gavin stood next to the desk, a look of surprise on his face as he looked from Siddhe to Rowen.

"I've come to see the captain. I've had another prophecy. I know how to help you get what you seek."

"Prophecy?" Elian's brows rose and he stood from his seat. "Let her go, Siddhe."

Siddhe pushed Rowen back and stepped aside. "This better be good," she murmured, looking Rowen up and down.

"Rowen," Elian said, his voice suspiciously tender. "Sit down, dear."

Rowen walked to the empty chair before his desk covered in open maps. She sat down and folded her hands in her lap. It was clear that whatever he sought was important to him, and this might be the leverage she needed to gain an edge on him.

She just couldn't tell him the true prophecy. Images of their dead bodies flashed before her eyes, turning her blood cold as the icicles that used to form outside her prison window.

Elian settled back in his seat. He nodded to her. "Go on, Rowen. Tell us what you saw. Don't leave out any detail."

Rowen started to speak, then snapped her mouth shut. She shot a nervous look at Gavin.

Damnation. She forgot to think of a fake prophecy.

"Uh," she fumbled, searching her mind for something of substance.

"Take your time," Elian said, calmly.

His soft voice eased her nerves but did nothing to help her think of a credible prophecy.

"Well," Rowen said, trying to buy herself time. She placed her hands on the table and smoothed the map before her. "You see. The images are a bit cloudy."

"Lying little whore," Siddhe growled.

Rowen began to speak again, and let out an ear-shattering cry as Siddhe stabbed a sharp knife into her hand, pinning it to the table.

The pain shot into her hand like fire.

Elian shot to his feet. "Siddhe!"

Gavin rushed to help Rowen free her hand.

Hysterical and in greater pain than she'd ever experienced, tears poured from Rowen's eyes.

"You! You bitch!" Rowen shouted, no longer caring about her regal upbringing.

The sight of her own flood pooling onto the Elian's maps made her lose all composure. Through a film of tears, she looked to Gavin who stood there, unsure of what to do.

"Help me!"

"Why did you do that?" Elian asked Siddhe, raking a hand through his blond hair. "You've ruined my maps!"

Siddhe stepped to him until they were face to face. "She's a blasted fake! You should be thanking me." She looked to Rowen and burst out laughing. "She deserves worse!"

"Bad call," Gavin said, his brows furrowing as he tried to remove the blade from the table.

Rowen cried out. Every inch the knife moved sent her closer to passing out from the pain.

"Move," Elian said, shoving Gavin aside. Without a second thought, he snatched the knife from the desk and threw it across the room, sending it straight into the wood of the door.

Rowen pulled her hand away and cradled it to her chest. Sobbing, she shot a glare at Siddhe. "You're insane!"

With a growl, Elian snatched the map from the table. "You'll pay for this with your hide," he said to Siddhe.

"You can try," Siddhe shot back.

Rowen looked to Elian and came to her feet. Freezing, her eyes went to the map that was half blank, and half finished. Her eyes widened as she took a closer look.

Her blood.

It trailed along the blank side of the map, creating images, symbols, and letters from a language she'd never seen.

Together, she and Elian raised the eyes to one another, their mouths open with shock.

"Bloody hell," Gavin said, blinking. "How'd she do that?"

The room fell silent as everyone turned to look at Rowen.

"She can't," Elian replied, looking at Rowen with curious eyes. He tilted his head. "Only the blood of a prophet from my family line can do such a thing."

Rowen shook her head. Despite the mind-numbing pain, Rowen couldn't take her eyes from the map as her blood filled in the drawings. When she dared to lift her eyes back to Elian's an odd half-smile rested on his lips.

"Daughter?"

Before Rowen could utter another word, a loud explosion sent them all to the floor as the ship rocked and shook.

CHAPTER TWENTY-THREE

ROWEN GASPED AS THE SHIP rocked and threw them all into the far wall.

"What's happening?" she asked with a wince as she landed on her wounded hand.

"I can take a guess," Siddhe said, scrambling to her feet. She glared at Elian. "What do you want to bet it's the Withraen Navy?"

"Damn," Elian growled. "We have to protect the ship."

Siddhe and Elian ran from the cabin, leaving Rowen and Gavin to collect themselves.

"Are you okay?" Gavin asked, helping Rowen to her feet.

Rowen groaned. "I could be better." She wobbled on her feet as the ship rocked and swayed. "Looks like they've come for me."

"Well, there's not exactly anywhere to run from here."

She turned to him. "Help me escape," she pleaded. "What do you have to lose? Get me a boat and help me get off this ship."

Gavin inhaled. "Rowen. I want to help you. Believe me. But, I don't know what I can do to help you."

Rowen winced as she held her wounded hand to her chest. She took Gavin's hand with her other, and pulled him from the cabin.

As she did so, she took another look at the map. Something told her that she couldn't leave it behind. If anything, it could be a bargaining chip. So, she grabbed it from the floor and stuffed it into her dress.

They ran from the cabin and into the hall. Rowen froze at hearing the roar of yells and canons on deck. This was going to be dangerous. But, she was ready. After Siddhe stabbed her in the hand, she didn't want to spend one more minute around her.

Then, there was the fact that Elian called her daughter.

That gave her pause.

What did he mean by that?

She cried out as a canon blew through the ship and soared past them, crashing into the wall just feet ahead of them.

Gavin grabbed her and pulled her out of the way as shards of wood and flames flew at their faces.

Rowen could barely catch her breath as they tumbled down the hall. They rolled and tumbled into the end of the hallway and into a wall.

"Come on," Gavin said, pulling her to her feet.

He grabbed her hand, and pulled her along. He ran much faster than her legs were willing to go. More blood dripped onto her soaking wet dress and onto the slick floor, and her mind whirled with pain. She fought through it, the adrenaline pumping through her veins. She skidded to a stop and beheld the open hole where the cannon had burst through. The choppy sea awaited outside, ready to suck them all up and never let go.

There was no way the ship was going to survive a blow such as that. As she stood at the edge, she thought of jumping. Rowen was a strong swimmer, but without a clue as to how far they were from land, she turned and ran to Gavin.

Once they reached the stairs that led up deck, Gavin slowed his pace and proceeded cautiously.

"What's going on up there?"

"Wait here," he said, holding his finger up to her lips to quiet her.

Rowen looked past him and her lips parted as she caught a glimpse of the sky for the first time in days. Arrows shot through the air, and to her utter terror, a large shining red dragon flew ahead and blew fire at the ship's sails. The flames' reach was incredible, striking with expert precision at every sail and pirate in its path.

Rowen groaned, almost losing her courage. Getting around him would be a challenge.

"Bloody hell," Gavin said. He looked back at her with a lifted brow. "Sure you want to try your luck on the sea alone?"

Rowen chewed her bottom lip and shrugged. "I'd rather that than to drown or be burnt alive."

That was all he needed to hear, and he made a run for the deck. Rowen mustered all of her courage and made a run to catch up. If they got separated, she didn't know what she would do.

The scene above deck was much worse than she expected. Her heart raced as she watched Withraen soldiers board the ship. Captain Elian—armed with a sword—was up top, shouting orders and fighting soldiers as fiercely as she'd seen any swordsman in the arenas of Withrae. He'd taken off his cloak, revealing strong arms and strange scars on his neck that she hadn't noticed before.

A loud battle cry caught Rowen's attention and she turned to see Siddhe fighting a group of uniformed soldiers. Her skin glowed and glittered like the sea under moonlight, and Rowen couldn't take her eyes off of her.

Siddhe was ruthless on deck, with two swords and a strength that matched the Dragon men. The other crew mates fought at her side. This was the first time she'd seen the other pirates in action, and to her surprise, they fought fiercely against the Dragons. Blood squirted from severed heads, and chopped off limbs, and the tide turned.

The Withraen soldiers were done fighting as men.

Terror struck Rowen's heart, and the hairs on her neck stood on end as the soldiers began to transform, into dragons of all sizes and colors.

The fair fight no longer existed. This was now an extermination. She gasped as she watched Siddhe jumped off the side of the ship and into the sea.

Rowen sucked in a breath as Gavin shook her. "This way," he said and turned the corner.

She followed, careful to keep cover against the side of the ship. Gavin led her to the boats and relief washed over her. She glanced over her shoulder for one last look at Elian and the others.

The humans wouldn't have a chance now that most of the Dragons shifted to their bestial form. She let out a loud scream as she and Gavin ran into a uniformed Withraen soldier, one of the last to shift. A wide smile came to his face as he realized who she was.

"You, prince killer," he said, licking his teeth. "Get over here before I have to come and get you."

Panicking, Rowen slapped a hand onto his face. She slapped much harder than she intended to, but fear gave her strength.

"Protect us," she ordered, clenching her teeth at the amount of energy she had to use on the burly Dragon. It rushed up from her belly and filled her arms and hands with a coolness that made a puff of cold air escape her lips. She was amazed by how different the sensation was for everyone.

Nodding, and slack-jaw, the soldier drew his sword. "Stay close," he said, and without further orders, he started slicing through his soldiers as they ran toward Gavin and Rowen.

Rowen shook Gavin. "Come on! Before they kill him."

Gavin nodded. "Impressive," he said.

"Maybe," Rowen said. "But, it won't last long."

They ran to the side of the ship where the smaller sail boats were strapped. Gavin rubbed his chin. "I don't know how to get one of these things into the water."

Rowen huffed and started tugging at the ropes, ignoring the pain in her hand. She pulled with all of her might. This was her last chance. She refused to return to Withrae.

Gavin sprang into action and took a knife from his boot. He started sawing at the thick ropes when the dragon flew in front of them.

Rowen gasped and backed away as flames spewed from the dragon's mouth, burning the ropes and the boats with it. She closed her eyes against the heat and used her hands to shield her face.

The Dragon growled at them. "No escape," he said. With a deep, rumbling chuckle, he flew away.

Cries of pain came from behind them. Rowen spun around to see that most of the crew lay lifeless on the floor, their arms and legs sprawled out in pools of blood. Her eyes went up to see Elian struggling to fight off two Dragons. He'd somehow created a shield to protect himself from the flames, and crouched low to concentrate his energy. That did nothing to protect his men.

Another canon shot into the ship and made it tilt to one side, knocking Rowen and Gavin from their feet. They caught onto the railing of the ship, and held on for their lives.

"Everything is falling apart," Gavin said, grimacing against the pain from his wounded shoulder.

"It seems that way," Rowen said, feeling the weight of her body pulling her down. She prayed that the ship would steady itself. Her mind raced for another escape route. Short of jumping overboard, she was stuck.

Her shoulders slumped.

She was going to die after all.

Rowen screamed as her hand slipped and sent her falling backward. Gavin gasped and reached for her, their fingers touching for a split second.

Her would spun as she fell from the ship and toward the sea.

This was it.

Death awaited, ready to claim for once and for all, when a pair of giant silver talons grabbed her by her shoulders, and lifted her into the sky.

The burning ship began the fade the higher she was taken into the sky.

Rowen's lips parted and she looked upward at the beautiful dragon that carried her away from what she was sure wouldn't be her last brush with death.

CHAPTER TWENTY-FOUR

STILL IN AWE, ROWEN COULDN'T take her eyes off of the magnificent dragon that saved her life. For a moment, she'd feared that it was just a soldier carrying her to the Withraen Navy's ship. Once both ships faded into the distance, she realized that this Dragon, with its shining black onyx scales, silver talons, a silver crest on his head, and silver ribbed wings couldn't have been a mere soldier.

It was her savior.

She took her eyes from him for a moment just to enjoy the feel of fresh air on her face. The scent of pine trees and salt water brought back many memories. The stench of the prison and the musky smell of her cabin prison were wiped clean of her flesh as she basked in the euphoria of freedom.

She closed her eyes and smiled, the sun beaming down on her face.

She made it. She wasn't completely safe yet, but the joy of being free from the ship and the pirates overwhelmed her to the brink of tears Her smile faded as a pang of guilt struck her heart. She just hoped that Gavin had survived.

She couldn't think of a way that he could. From the looks of it, they all seemed to be facing a bitter end.

Her legs dangled beneath her and the wind picked up as the Dragon gained speed.

When she opened her eyes, she recognized the dock ahead of them. Bustling, and lively with sailors, ships, and boats, Rowen realized that Logan was right.

This was Harrow.

This was home.

"Who are you?" Rowen shouted above the roar of wind that swept around her. "Why are you saving me?"

The Dragon glanced down at her, but kept silent.

"Aren't you going to say something?"

They reached the port of Harrow and the Dragon flew right past it to a clearing in the woods that awaited just near the main road to the market.

Without a word, or a warning, the Dragon lowered itself to the ground, and let her go. It was all very unceremonious and disappointing, but she wasn't going to complain.

Rowen scrambled to her feet and turned to the Dragon. He outstretched his beautiful black wings and lifted himself back into the air.

And, without a goodbye, he flew away.

Rowen was left dumbstruck.

Who was he?

The question fleeted almost as quickly as it popped into her head as she realized something.

She was alone. She had no money.

And, worst of all, she had nowhere to hide.

Rowen spun around and took in her surroundings. The road led from the port to the city of Harrow. The woods led to another road that would take her to the border that separated the Dragon realm from the human realm.

The pain of her hand left her weak. She needed new clothes and a new identity.

What would she do, now? She couldn't go home to the Duke.

Rowen closed her eyes and took in a deep breath.

She would do all that she could.

She checked that the map was still in the front of her dress, and ran.

CHAPTER TWENTY FIVE

PRINCE RICKARD LINGERED ABOVE THE clouds, his eyes fixed on the half-blood dragon girl below.

With the sun on his back, and the city of Harrow below, he was at peace with his decision. Shielding Rowen from the prison torturer had been easy.

A bribe.

A promise of a title.

Easy.

Rickard even had a plan to save her from the gallows, a plan that had been thwarted quite conveniently.

Then, there was the burning ship rescue with the Withraen navy there to witness it all. That had been a bit trickier.

Rickard pumped his wings and steadied himself in the sky. To touch her once more was out of the question. To reveal himself for what he really was had to wait.

It seemed that everything he did was to protect her, even from the truths she was not ready to learn. Watching her run into the woods sent a pain into his heart. Her journey would be hard, and he wouldn't be able to always save her.

Now, she would be on her own.

With a sigh that produced a puff of smoke from his nostrils, Rickard abandoned going back to the Withrae Navy ship that had led him to Rowen, and flew back toward his castle.

His brother was dead.

His father was ill.

Soon, he would rule all of Withrae. And, soon he would be faced with righting all of the wrong his father and brother had done.

Just a little while longer to keep his plan a secret.

Just a while longer to let her continue hating him.

Rickard flew over Harrow and made one last stop. He landed on a merchant road and shifted back to his human form. Dressed in the same simple cloak over leather pants and a plain shirt, he would blend in with the common crowd. He didn't need any Dragons recognizing him and ruining his plans.

A manor built of gray stone awaited up ahead, one that he had visited a few times before. Always in secret.

Glenick Manor.

Rickard walked along the rocky road and toward the iron front gate. There she was, his accomplice. She waited for him, her hands before her, red, and nearly wrung raw.

When her golden eyes caught a glimpse of him, she ran to the gate and wrapped her hands around the bars.

"Prince Rickard," Duchess Nimah Glenick breathed with relief. "Tell me what has happened."

He placed a finger to his lips and stood before her. "Shh. Don't call me that. You know better."

Nimah nodded, her eyes darting from side to side and back up the white path that led to the manor she shared with her ridiculous husband.

"Is she okay?" she asked, her face pale, her eyes wide with worry. "I haven't been able to sleep in days. Please tell me she's alive."

Rickard nodded. "She is. I made sure of it. But, I can't do much to help her now. She will have to protect herself until I am king."

Nimah's eyes watered and she covered her face with her hands. "I shouldn't have allowed her to go. I should have kept her here with me and out of all of this."

"No," Rickard said. "You did the right thing."

"But, she can't even come home to me. She knows nothing of what the world holds and what dangers await. I should be there with her."

Rickard's jaw tensed. "No," he said, lowering his voice. "You will stick to the plan, keep your mouth shut, and wait for my word. Don't get sloppy and ruin everything. Understand?"

Nimah sucked up her tears, looked him in the eyes, and nodded.

"Did you manage to make sense of what Elian's old scribe sent in the message?"

Rickard shook his head. "Elian killed him before I could transcribe everything. Something about the map isn't working anymore. The rest is what we already knew. He's after the Red Dragon."

Nimah huffed, a look of bitterness creasing her brows. "He's always been after it. It's all he cares about."

"Do you think he knows that Rowen is his?"

"I don't know. I never told him. I can't believe he showed up and rescued her. He's always been full of surprises."

Rickard scratched his bearded chin. Itchy. Rough. It was time to shave it off and start anew. "At least something worked in our favor," he said.

His ears picked up the sound of footsteps coming from afar. Riding boots crunching on leaves and then the flat stone walkway.

The Duke.

Rickard took Nimah's hand from between the bars. "I must go. Trust me. She's strong, stronger than we gave her credit for. She will survive, and I will always be there for her if I can."

Nimah nodded. "Thank you, Rickard. She's lucky to have you."

Rickard twisted his mouth. "Luck?" he asked. "Never believed in it."

Then, he shifted, and took to the skies.

The plan was in place. The prophecies were going as foretold. And, the woman he'd chosen as his mate was alive.

That's all that mattered.

For now.

Thanks for reading! If you enjoyed this book, please consider leaving a review.

An Exclusive Excerpt from Rise of the Flame

CHAPTER ONE

LILAE FLOATED BARE-SKINNED BENEATH THE bright crescent moon, her arms outstretched on the lake's calm surface. Winter never seemed to end in northern Eura, but she braved the frigid water for the solitude offered by an evening swim.

Alone, she thought, just how I like it.

Just as she began to relax, Lilae felt the presence of her Elder in the black shadows of the forest.

This is not good. She peeked over and saw Delia in the human form she'd stolen when she was forced to leave the Underworld, her pale face illuminated from beneath the hood of her wool cloak. She held her wooden staff in one hand and Lilae's discarded cloak in the other.

"Lilae!"

Lilae swallowed and then flipped over to swim back toward the shore, closing the gap between them. She quickly got out of the water and dressed, taking the heavy cloak from Delia's grasp and flinging it over her shoulders to ward off the chill in the air.

"What is it? What's happened?" Her breath escaped her lips like a puff of smoke in the darkness.

Delia looked over Lilae with dull blue eyes. "I don't like how close they are getting. We need to leave before dawn."

Lilae tucked her boyish pants into her boots. Only a few years ago, she would have refused; she would have run away to stay with another family in their village. Now, at almost eighteen, Lilae resigned herself to their nomadic lifestyle.

That's because she had finally learned why they moved so much: Lilae was being hunted.

Lilae followed Delia through the forest to their little cottage on the edge of town. It was a small structure, built into the side of a hill. Though it was once a cave, Pirin had made it into a real home. A squat chimney protruded from beneath the soil, a trail of smoke wafting from its mouth into the gray sky.

Ducking, Lilae stepped inside. Pirin, Lhana, and the twins, Risa and Jaiza, were already awake. Her surrogate family. They glanced at her and, without a word, returned to their preparations. They all moved slowly as the cold air in the room bit at them.

Pirin put his arm around Lhana. She stopped packing and buried her tears in his shoulder, sighing. "Just tell me why? Every time we finally get comfortable and make friends, you make us leave."

He smoothed her blonde hair and kissed her cheek. "And every time you ask me this same question. The answer will not change. They are coming. We don't have time to waste."

"Let us stay behind. It's not the girls and me that he wants."

Pirin grabbed Lhana by the elbow. The room fell silent, and Lilae tensed, her eyes darting from Lhana's stunned face to Pirin's stern expression.

Pirin lowered his voice, but Lilae heard every word. "We stay together. She is my responsibility."

Lhana swallowed and arched a brow, her jaw clenched. Her eyes may have glared in defiance, but her voice wavered. "I thought she was the Elder's responsibility. You trained her. Your duty is done."

Pirin pulled Lhana closer. "I will not hear another word about it." The discussion was over. Pirin's word was law. Everyone went back to packing.

Lilae glanced at Lhana and wondered if the Ancients knew how much Lhana hated her. Lhana met Lilae's eyes, her blond brows furrowing. It was a look that hurt Lilae more than anything; there was almost nothing she wanted more than to finally feel that woman's love.

Despite the tension, they all enjoyed a hasty breakfast of buttered toast, eggs, and fried potatoes, aware that this might be the last they would have for quite some time. They all ate silently and packed their leftovers in sacks. Lhana also packed dried toast and fruit for the journey. They would have to buy more supplies as they went on or rely on Pirin to hunt while in the wilderness.

While the others gathered their belongings, Lilae sharpened her dagger. For her, packing was always quick. She had nothing of value. She wore her only trinket of worth around her neck. It was a simple silver necklace with shiny stones around a ruby. Besides that, a sack of clothing and an extra pair of boots was all Lilae needed.

Jaiza's grunt sounded like exasperation as she stuffed her favorite dress into her travel bag. She reached for her bow and arrows and headed toward the door, not even looking at Lilae as she passed by.

Once everyone was ready, Lilae hooded herself and followed the procession into the woods. Soon, the sun would rise, and farmers would tend to their cattle and crops.

Delia led the way as they quietly crossed the village to the path leading east. Always east. She cut through the darkness, taking them from gentle paths directly into the thickness of the woods, where the grass was knee high and the hungry bugs were ready to feast on any exposed skin they could find. They were all used to it by now. It would be just another long, hard journey to a foreign land.

Whenever she saw Delia look into the sky, eyes glowing and staff raised, she imagined that she could actually see the Ancients peering down at them from their homes in the Overworld. When Lilae glanced upward, she saw only stars.

"I am glad we have a moment to speak, Lilae. I've been wondering how you feel, now that you're approaching your eighteenth birthday."

"I feel fine." She stuffed her gloved hands into her pockets to warm them. "I am ready for a new journey. I feel more at peace in the wilderness. No one can be mean to me out here, and no one can hurt me." She shrugged it off and forced a smile Delia's way. She didn't want to complain.

"No one can hurt you, Lilae," Delia said, "unless you let them. Have The Winds spoken to you lately?"

"No, they have been quiet."

"Well. Perhaps it is a good thing. They warn you of danger that even I cannot see."

Lilae nodded. "Yes. I don't need The Winds to tell to look out for boys. I'm glad to be free of Jameson's taunting."

"Tell me about this boy."

"He smells like the pigs and always tries to wrestle me in the pits." Lilae scrunched up her nose. "I won't wrestle him, even if I want to twist his arm off."

Delia chuckled softly as she glanced at her. "I'm glad to hear it. I hope you know he wants more than to wrestle, Lilae. I'm sure he fancied you."

"Gross."

"Risa and Jaiza enjoy the company of boys. I'm sure they are ready for marriage, but you know you're different, right?"

"I know. I guess I don't care about the same things that they do. I do not care about friends or boys or starting a family of my own."

A small smile formed on Delia's lips. "Of course not..." She winked at Lilae. "—you're too young to think of such things."

"Am I?" She couldn't see a boy falling in love with her or raising children of her own. But that didn't mean she wouldn't like an adoring, handsome boy professing his love to her; she just didn't think that it was possible. She looked odd. She acted differently. It was better not to dream about such things.

"Don't most girls get married at my age?" She stepped over a fallen tree and waited for the others to do the same.

The grass grew taller, nearing their necks. It was covered in ice, making it so sharp that they had to walk through it with caution. So many years of walking, of moving. When would they stop?

"Sure, some do. There are scores of young girls who, at the first sign of womanhood, begin bearing children, too. And they will do so continuously until the seed no longer catches. But that's not the life for you. You have a future, Lilae. There's a bigger, more important task for you than just producing babies. You are different."

"How? Why? Because there's something wrong with me?"

"No!" Delia waved a flippant hand and peered at Lilae. "Nonsense. There's nothing wrong with you. You're special. You have a very important destiny."

"But why, Delia?" For as long as she could remember, she just went with whatever Delia or Pirin said was best. "How am I special? Why am I being hunted? I've never hurt anyone innocent. I have killed, but I follow the judgment of The Winds."

Delia was silent for a moment. "Soon," she said and patted Lilae on the shoulder.

"She is ready," Lilae heard Delia whisper to herself as if praying to the Ancients above.

CHAPTER TWO

WEEKS HAD PASSED SINCE LILAE and the others had seen another village. They kept off the worn paths and stayed as close to The Barrier as possible. The massive stone structure stood as a constant reminder that they were far from civilization. No one ventured near The Barrier; it was feared.

As they climbed over foothills and through mountain passes, Lilae glanced at the top of The Barrier, where a green haze rippled from the top of the stone to the clouds. She hoped that she'd catch a glimpse of a Silver Elf. Silver Elves shared a wall with the humans, and, in her mind, they were the friendliest of the six remaining races.

The terrain changed from treacherous mountains and valleys, where the snow and wind whipped past their nearly frozen faces, to smooth plains and dense forests. It was like a dream to see the different landforms of Eura.

They crossed over a bridge that connected two massive mountains. When they reached the top, it felt as if they were in the clouds. Whenever Lilae had the nerve to look down, all she saw was a white mist that resembled smoke. Though she couldn't see it, she knew that a river rushed through the valley below. Its waters crashed along the rocks, causing a deafening roar to fill the valley.

Too high, Lilae thought. The wind whipped around her, making her red hair fly into her eyes.

Lilae gulped and tried to catch her breath. Her hands started to shake as she imagined herself plummeting to her death. She hoped the bridge was sturdy enough to support them. Her hands gripped the rough ropes that served as railings so tightly that they cut into the palms of her hands.

Lilae was usually at the head of the pack, but now, she was the last to gather the nerve to cross. She willed herself to move her feet, forcing her mind to stop feeding her images of falling and hitting her head on every rock that lay below.

Her breath sped up. The slats of the bridge were cracking; some were already missing. She looked to Pirin with terrified eyes.

He seemed too far away. Lilae saw him motion for her to cross.

"You can do it, Lilae," Pirin yelled above the roar of the river below.

Lilae looked down again, the mist curling up around her ankles.

"Just take your time."

His patience with her gave her courage. She nodded, more to convince herself that she was ready than anything else.

Lilae took a deep breath and headed toward Pirin. She would hate for him to think of her as a coward. She walked carefully across, praying the entire time. She drew a breath of relief when she safely reached the other side and joined the others.

They began down a steep trail that led back into the wilderness. They were all tired. Everyone was moody. Risa and Jaiza stayed close to each other, as always, and looked simply miserable.

Lilae walked ahead of them all, trapped in her thoughts, clinging to her more pleasant dreams to keep her going. Hunger nagged at her stomach. Her feet were calloused and sore from hundreds of miles of walking. Still, she refused to complain.

Pirin once told her that complaints and excuses were signs of weakness. From as early as she could remember, his words were like law, and she lived by his and Delia's teachings.

"Please, Pirin." Lhana stopped abruptly. She breathed heavily, coughing from the cold in the air. She dropped her bags onto the ground with a thud and folded her arms across her chest. "We have been walking since dawn and without a decent break. I am exhausted." Her shoulders slumped. "Please, darling, can we rest now?"

Pirin gave her one look. She was pale, her cheeks red from the wind. There was a small clearing at the mouth of a cavern. He looked to Delia.

The Elder placed her staff on the ground, looked around, and nodded her approval.

That's how it always was: Pirin checking to make sure Delia was in agreement. He shrugged his heavy pack off of his back and held it with one hand.

He nodded toward the cave. Lilae looked at it. It was a small opening in the side of the gray mountain, and all she could see was black inside. She was glad that she wasn't as afraid of the dark as she was of heights.

"This way," Pirin said, leading them to the clearing. They climbed the rocks and heaved their sacks inside the shelter. "This will suffice for the night."

There was a collective sigh of relief and everyone busied themselves with setting up camp inside the hollow mouth of the cave. They would make it as comfortable as possible.

"Looks like rain anyway," Pirin said and peered into the night sky. He sniffed the air. "I'm sure of it. Build a fire inside the cave and we'll sleep there."

"How long can we stay?" Lhana wrapped her arms around his waist.

Pirin looked at Risa. "Until morning."

Jaiza's gaze went to the dark woods on the other side of the cave. "But what about wolves? I saw at least three carcasses on the way up here."

"We'll make a fire. Don't worry," Pirin assured her. "Lilae, go out and place the rabbit traps."

Lilae nodded, uncaring about the cold; it never affected her as it did the others. She wanted to talk further with Delia. Their nights beside the fire, learning and hearing stories, were what Lilae looked forward to each day.

"Who will keep watch?" Jaiza eyed the dark cave and then the forest again. If there was one thing that Jaiza was afraid of, it was wolves.

Pirin had already started to gather wood from fallen branches around the camp. "I'll watch for half of the night, and then you girls can take turns. We'll get horses from the next village and I promise we can stay at an inn."

The twins smiled. Lilae watched their faces light up, and it brought a small smile to her lips. The thought of sleeping in an inn excited them all. There, they could drink ale and meet new people. The food was always hearty, even if the beds were sometimes infested with bed bugs.

Lilae lingered near the slope into the woods while the others set up. She heard something. Her head tilted as she listened to The Winds.

Delia looked back at her, concern spreading across her face. "What is it, Lilae?"

Lilae held a gloved hand up and continued to listen. The Winds spoke to her. They were always there like an old friend. The voices that floated along the breeze or rushing winds always warned her when something was amiss. She had relied on them since she was a child, and they never lied.

Now, they issued a warning.

"Bandits," Lilae said, standing tall. Her eyes searched for movement in the bushes.

"Oh, great. She's talking to herself again," Risa whispered.

"Shush, Risa." Jaiza nudged her sister's arm. "She may talk to herself, but has she ever been wrong?"

Risa didn't reply. They both watched as Lilae stood near the edge of the woods.

"Murderers." The Winds were sure to tell Lilae that, and she gave the twins a look that they understood.

"They followed our tracks, and they wish to rob and kill us," Lilae said it as if she was discussing the weather.

"Humph. I wish they'd try," Jaiza said with a glower in the same direction as Lilae's gaze.

Delia drew in a deep breath. "Holy Elahe. We can never travel in peace?" She stabbed her staff into the ground. "Those bandits are damned fools to be this close to The Barrier."

"I don't like this." Lhana's eyes darted toward the forest as she withdrew to hide near the cave. "Why does this always happen? One day they'll sneak up on us, I just know it!"

"I won't let that happen," Lilae said, glancing back at her.

"You will be the death of me," Lhana said as she turned her back on Lilae.

Pirin gave her a sidelong glance. "Perhaps you'd let me train you some time, Lhana. You are not as defenseless as you pretend to be. Your trait is quite rare—it could be of use to us."

Lhana glared at him. "I don't want to hear it. You seem to forget that I am a proper lady. Only warriors use their traits."

Pirin shrugged. "Suit yourself. I don't understand why you'd rather waste something you've inherited."

Lhana shook her head. "Never. So stop asking me." She raised a finger. "The first queen of the black throne gave my family my dowry. Who else can make such a claim?"

Risa sighed and gave Jaiza a look. They both set their things down without a word. They'd trained with Lilae for times such as this since they were all children, and this wouldn't be the first group of bandits to threaten them.

Jaiza grabbed her bow, securing her quiver of arrows onto her back.

Risa drew her sword quietly and put the scabbard down. She rolled her shoulders as if loosening her muscles.

Lilae grinned, her teeth shining in the moonlight. She loved when the twins were like this.

Jaiza stepped beside Lilae, who was younger yet taller. Her keen eyes looked into the growing darkness. "I'll go ahead and see how many there are." She twisted her blonde hair into a knot at the top of her head to keep it from getting in the way.

"There are eight."

"You know everything, don't you?" Jaiza rolled her eyes. "Fine. I can take them out."

Lilae's grin widened. The thrill of a fight excited her. "I'll be right behind you."

Pirin continued to unpack their supplies, shaking out their wool blankets. "This will be good practice for you girls. It's been awhile since you've had a real fight. Maybe you can practice working as a team this time..."

Risa lowered her sword. "Eight? What a waste of energy."

Pirin gave her a stern look.

"What? I was hoping for at least ten," she said as though it was a sport. "That would have been good practice. I can handle eight on my own." She put her sword away and started to help Lhana prepare the salted pork and beans.

"Risa..."

"Father..." Risa said as she squatted down and pulled out an iron pot. "Lilae and Jaiza can take this one."

"Don't be so cocky. You're not the best fighter in the realm by any stretch of the imagination, so stop acting like you know everything. Even your Evasion can be countered if someone has the right skill. Trust me, killing people isn't a game and should not be taken lightly."

Risa raised a brow. "I know it isn't. But Lilae and Jaiza can handle it. We've done this how many times now? At least seven."

"Never underestimate your enemy, Risa. You never know if those men are as trained as you or better."

"You can't be serious." Risa huffed. "I doubt it. We both know that most bandits are nothing more than boys who can barely hold the weight of their own cheap sword."

"You're not listening, are you?"

"Yes, Father. I get what you're saying. I will try not to be so cocky about it. That better?"

Pirin sighed. "You girls are impossible," he said, though a small smile played across his lips.

"You didn't train us to be warriors for nothing," Risa said, as Jaiza slunk into the forest.

Without a sound, Jaiza climbed into a tall tree and disappeared into the branches and leaves.

Lilae stepped out of her cloak with her dagger sharpened and ready in one hand. It was warm on her palm and pulsed for action. She listened to The Winds as they led her to the men who approached her family's camp, careful not to crunch any of the fallen branches beneath her feet.

As the sun's last light faded, she peered silently at the bandits from her place behind a tall oak tree. Energy flowed within her body, and there was an anxiousness filling her throat and a fire within her veins.

The Winds warned her that the men were merciless. They preyed on innocent travelers, robbing and killing even defenseless women. In return, Lilae and Jaiza would show no mercy.

There was a sudden whistling sound as Jaiza's arrow cut through the dark forest and slammed into the chest of the leader. He gasped loudly, clutching his chest as he was thrown back onto the ground with a solid thud. The arrow was made of the strongest wood and impaled him to the dirt so that he couldn't lift himself.

Lilae noted the look of shock and pain on his face as he strained against the arrow. That look always interested her. It was the look of one surprised by death's touch.

Shouts and frantic orders ensued from the other bandits as they drew their weapons and searched for the source of the arrow. They held their weapons but ducked and cowered toward the safety of the dense, dark forest.

Lilae watched them in silence. She could feel their fear, knowing their hearts were thumping with the terror of the unknown. She wanted them to feel that fear. It was the same fear countless others had felt when those men harmed them. Risa was right about one thing: their weapons were cheap. But these were not boys; they were men who had done this countless times, with success. This would be their last.

"Who's there?" someone shouted in a high-pitched voice that cracked with his words.

"Demons!" another wailed.

"Shut up, Gred. There ain't no stupid demons in this forest!" Lilae heard someone reply, yet she could hear the fear in his voice as if he were uncertain about his own reassurances.

"I told you we shouldn't tempt the Ancients! We're too close to The Barrier!"

Lilae worked quickly, hoping to get some action before Jaiza killed them all with her skilled archery. She took a deep breath, and her vision changed. She could see their moves before they even did them. Everything stilled for her; all sounds muted, and Lilae activated her Focus.

Silence welcome Lilae as she raced into the battle, calculating their every action.

She darted into the mob with her dagger in her fist. She sliced Gred down before he even saw her coming. Lilae didn't waste time making sure he was dead. Her dagger had cut his throat with such precision that there were no doubts.

She slammed into a tall, burly man who seemed more like a solid tree. His body was made of pure muscle, hard as stone. Lilae climbed his body and stabbed him in the neck. Blood spurted into the air.

As he fell backward, his hands racing to cover his wound, she hopped from his body and went on to the next. She didn't need to look back; Lilae always struck true. She could hear him gasping for breath.

Someone grabbed Lilae by her hair from behind. She used her Evasion. Her image flickered before his eyes, and, in an instant, she yanked herself free from his grasp. She kicked him in the back with such force that she heard his spine crack.

His scream resonated throughout the woods, and Lilae put him out of his misery, pouncing onto his back. Her hands were secure against his thick, coarse beard as she snapped his neck.

She stood and turned around. The remaining men were lying on the ground, covered in blood and dirt. Jaiza's arrows protruded from their bodies. Lilae calmed her breathing.

She stood at the center of the massacre. Her eyes closed as she listened to the last groans of pain and gurgles of blood coming from the bandits' mouths. Her Focus subsided, and her vision of the world returned to normal.

Lilae waited until their sounds of dying ceased before making her way back to the camp. She emerged from the forest, her hands and clothes covered in blood splatters. She wiped her face free of a few speckles with a rag that Risa handed her.

Everyone stared at Lilae across the dancing flames as she warmed her bloodstained hands over the burning logs. Her pale face was streaked with blood, and her eyes watched the fire without a trace of emotion.

CHAPTER THREE

THE RAIN POURED OUTSIDE THE mouth of the cave. Its song was soothing, dripping steadily onto the stones. Lilae enjoyed such private moments with Delia. While the twins had their mother, Lilae had Delia. She still wondered why Lhana had shed that tear earlier. She sensed a deep sadness hidden within that woman.

Lilae sighed, snuggling closer to Delia with her wool blanket. Lilae rested her head on Delia's soft shoulder. She always smelled like mint from the oils she used.

Lilae broke the silence. "Why exactly am I different, Delia?" She had been waiting to ask that question for years now. It was always in her mind. From kingdom to kingdom, she never fit in. "Or special, as you say. Even more importantly, Delia, why is someone hunting me? Why would anyone want me dead?"

For as long as she could remember, Delia and Pirin had only told her the same thing: Someone very bad is after you and will stop at nothing to accomplish his task.

Delia looked down at Lilae as if considering what to tell her first. "They don't necessarily want you dead, Lilae. They want something from you." She sighed at the perplexed look that Lilae knew crossed her face. "I suppose you're ready."

Delia rose to her feet and held a hand out for Lilae. Lilae accepted the help and stood beside her. Delia was a small woman but that never made Lilae respect her any less. She looked on curiously as Delia held her willow staff out toward the mouth of the cave. A ripple of air floated from the staff and spread. A pale blue light connected to the ripples of air. It covered the entire opening of the cave like a sheer film.

The cave grew warm as if the film stood as a door that closed them inside. Lilae shrugged off her blanket and perked to attention.

"Let's go." She headed toward the ripples of air and stepped through.

Lilae hesitated for a moment, and Delia waved her forward. "Come," she whispered.

She could see Delia through the film. She reached a hand out first, and her body turned frigid. It felt as if a million thorns pricked her flesh, and she winced. She saw Delia standing on the other side, waiting patiently.

"Don't be afraid. It only stings for a second. The shield will not harm any of us. It is laced to shock anyone or anything that I have not named to protect. Do not worry."

She took Lilae's hand and pulled the rest of her body through. Delia walked into the darkness of the forest, expecting

Lilae to follow. She held her staff before her, leading the way. Lilae was surprised that they walked deeper and deeper into the forest.

The rain stopped but the ground was muddy and squishy beneath their boots. She could barely see ahead of her. She was afraid that they were being watched, yet The Winds were silent.

Lilae held on to Delia's small waist to keep from falling over. They walked for what felt like hours, and Lilae fought to keep her questions to herself. She could feel that it was time. Finally, she would know who she was, and what her future held. They stopped by a body of water.

Lilae stared at the lake, feeling the cold air drift closer to her. The soft patter of drizzle sprinkled onto its surface, bathed in moonlight. Lilae held her hand out, catching a cool droplet of water in her palm.

Delia walked to the edge of the water and waved her closer. "Kneel."

Lilae took off her boots and stepped closer. She loved the feel of the mud on her feet and stepped close enough for the water to lap over her toes. She knelt down beside the lake and looked up at Delia.

"Good. Now bow your head and close your eyes."

Lilae breathed deeply and looked out over the water. She bowed her head, and her eyes fluttered closed. Lilae nearly choked as she was grabbed violently and dragged into the water.

Lilae's eyes popped open as the water slapped her face. All she saw was darkness. Her mouth filled with water; she quickly tried to push the liquid out and close her mouth.

She could hold her breath for only so long, and her entire body froze with fear as something held her hand and pulled her deeper and deeper into the water. Lilae fought the urge to scream. Whatever held on to her was rough and unyielding. She could feel the hate and evil radiating from it. She fought to see ahead of her. She wanted to see what had hold of her, but all she saw before her were the inky depths of the lake.

Her ears filled with fluid and her eyes began to burn. Two yellow eyes glowed back at her, and Lilae felt her body shake.

She screamed. "Delia!"

Water flooded every orifice, and she panicked. She tried to regain her composure, but those eyes bore into hers. A hand went over her mouth and pressed her face deeper into the water until her head scraped the bottom of the lake.

Lilae flailed and fought. She needed air. Her mind became a torrent of screams and pleas. Her lungs burned. Her nose burned. Her heart thumped so fast that she was sure it would explode. And then, she saw a face. Bronze skin, yellow eyes that glowed beneath the water, and high cheekbones. Terror filled her very bones, creeping into her soul.

"Join me, Lilae. Or die," the creature said in a voice that was unlike anything Lilae had ever heard. It wasn't human; it had to be some sort of a demon from the Underworld.

Lilae shook her head. She felt lightheaded as if she was dying. Still, she refused.

"No!" She swallowed more water. She reached past the face and toward the surface. She could see the light. She craved it.

"Join me and I will ease your pain."

"No!"

Pain jolted through her body like a flood of hot acid.

"Then, your fate it sealed. You will be mine whether you choose to or not."

Like a slap to the face, Lilae was jolted back to the surface. Delia had her by her shirt's collar. She leaned over Lilae, closely watching for her reaction. Lilae coughed and choked as air flooded into her lungs. Cool, delicious air. She breathed it in greedily. She saw Delia nod with approval and sit back on her heels. She wrapped Lilae in her cloak, giving her a moment to calm down.

"What was that?" Lilae shrieked.

Delia put her hand out. "Quiet your voice."

Lilae shot to her feet, flinging off the cloak. She looked over at the lake. It was still now, peaceful. She would never look at water the same way.

Lilae's face heated, and tears stung her eyes. She had thought that she was going to die under the lake's surface; she never wanted to feel that way again. Lilae looked at Delia as tears slipped down her cheeks. She wiped furiously at them.

"What was that, Delia?"

Delia picked up the cloak off the ground and draped it over Lilae's shoulders. "First, tell me your choice. Did you choose to side with him?

"Who was that?"

"Answer the question, Lilae. It's important!"

Confused, Lilae tried to gather her thoughts. Wiping her face she shook her head. "I told him no."

Delia closed her eyes and let out a breath of relief. "Good girl. There is still hope then." She opened her eyes and pulled Lilae in for a hug.

Lilae buried her face in the warmth of Delia's chest. The comfort of her embrace still didn't banish the fear that threatened to make her cry out in hysterics.

"That was an apparition of the Ancient, Wexcyn. He has returned from his imprisonment in the abyss. He has come to claim his throne. And now, he knows that you cannot be swayed to fight on his side. You have denied him."

Lilae pulled away from Delia. That name did not sound familiar. She shook her head. "I don't understand." Cold water dripped from her clothes. She pulled the cloak closer to warm herself. She shivered and slumped to the ground, resting her back on a smooth cluster of rocks.

Her gaze went back to the water, and her eyes glazed over as she recalled the terror she had just experienced. There was a time when Lilae thought that she feared nothing.

Delia made a fire with the tip of her staff onto a rock. Lilae glanced over her shoulder. Such a fire was not possible, but Delia had a talent for the impossible.

Sitting beside Lilae, Delia put a hand on her shoulder and stroked it tenderly. "I'm sorry, Lilae, but I had to show you. Showing you what evil we are up against is better than just telling you. I find it much more effective."

Lilae scoffed. "It was quite effective, Delia. And it was uncalled for."

"I don't think so, Lilae. Wexcyn is a threat to everything you know and love."

"Was that real?"

"It was." Delia looked up at the stars. "It was real in your mind. I could see nothing of the encounter, but that doesn't mean that it didn't happen. Wexcyn invaded your thoughts. We are lucky that he is not strong enough to actually harm you from a distance. But soon, anything will be possible."

"Who is Wexcyn?"

Delia pulled her journal from her bag. It was a small book made of supple leather and filled with parchment.

It was the book Delia used to teach Lilae ever since Lilae was a child. There were ancient maps, history lessons, illustrations, and prophecies. Delia licked her thumb and flipped through a couple of weathered pages; she held open a page with a map on it. The map was drawn with such precision that Lilae wondered if Delia was an artist and had done it herself.

"You know about the four realms, Lilae, right?"

Lilae nodded. As a child, she had loved to learn and recite what she memorized. It was rare for anyone other than royalty and nobility to even be able to read. "Yes, of course. There's Eura, the human realm. Alfheim, the Silver Elf realm. Kyril, the Tryan realm. And Nostfar, the Shadow Elf realm."

Delia smiled. She smoothed a wild ringlet of Lilae's hair behind her ear. "Good girl. And who created the races?"

"Delia, we have traveled for as long as I can remember, and I've never heard anyone even mention the other races. Why is that?"

"Because it has been so long since anyone has seen someone from another race that it simply isn't thought about anymore. Can you tell me who created the remaining races?"

"Pyrii created the Tryans, Inora created the Shadow Elves, Ulsia the Silver Elves, and Telryd created the humans." Then, Lilae lifted an eyebrow. "You said... the remaining races. There were others?"

"Yes. Lord Elahe, the creator of the entire universe, created many Ancients to start new worlds... But we'll get to that another day. I am afraid I don't have time to explain the origins of the universe quite yet."

"But the others?" Lilae persisted. "What happened to them?"

Delia pointed to the lines that separated each realm from one another.

"The Barriers," she explained, "were created by the Ancients to keep us from warring with each other. When they created the different races, it was glorious. First, there was peace, and they were pleased. However, everything changed... when death was discovered. With the first death, the perfect world they had created and loved started to crumble. Quests for power and greed took over. Evil was born, and it infected some of the Ancients as well. Things were so bad when all of the races lived together that they almost destroyed our world." Delia turned the page to a picture of the Ancients.

"The Ancients created The Barriers to keep us safe from one another's powers, to return the world to balance."

Lilae examined the drawing of the Ancients.

Delia pointed to a picture of what resembled a man, except he seemed to be made of some type of metal.

He sat on a dark throne with a long spear in his hand and an intense look on his bronze face. Even as a picture, he seemed to stare back at Lilae, looking into her soul. She shivered and turned her eyes to the fire, scooting closer to Delia for warmth and protection. Before that night, Lilae thought that she feared nothing; she now feared Wexcyn with every fiber of her being.

"Wexcyn was the first Ancient created by Elahe. He was so powerful that his creations were able to manipulate any power that the other races could. He was almost too powerful, and he knew it. He wanted to rule his brothers and sisters. He wanted to be God."

"What Ancient was he, Delia? Who were his people?"

"They were called Mithrani. They were a beautiful race."

"And now they are all gone?"

"After the war, they hid. They are out there... Somewhere. And he was imprisoned in the abyss for his crimes. Wexcyn started an alliance with a few of the other Ancients. What they did in the Great War changed everything. They discovered something that threatened the entire world."

Lilae sat up straighter. She could picture everything Delia spoke of. The races, the gods, the war. "What happened? What did they change?"

"They discovered that each death of an individual makes their Ancient weaker."

Lilae nodded. "It makes sense," she said and ran a finger across her bottom lip as she thought. "Delia... the Great War wasn't about us, was it? It was really a fight between the Ancients?"

"Indeed."

Lilae stared at the picture again. Those eyes would haunt her until the day she died. He had once been the most powerful Ancient in existence. What would he do to her if he was close enough? He resembled a human, yet he seemed to be a supernaturally enhanced version. Seeing him hold that golden spear worried her. She could picture that spear impaling her.

Lilae furrowed her eyebrows as she looked at his picture. "Is that what is coming, Delia? Another war?"

"They have already taken sides, my dear. This war has been brewing for ages. I am afraid we can no longer avoid it. The Ancients knew that Wexcyn couldn't stay imprisoned forever.

He has too many supporters who have been trying to free him for centuries."

Lilae looked at the sky, imagining as she always did that she could see the Ancients up there in the Overworld. "And who is on our side, Delia?"

"The odds are in our favor... for now. Telryd, Ulsia, and Pyrii fight for life, for the preservation of this world."

"So that leaves Inora, the Shadow Elves' Ancient. She betrayed us, then."

"I wish it were that easy, Lilae. I really do. I fear the other Ancients have returned, as well. There are races that you've never even heard of, hiding out there... ready for revenge."

"Bellens, you mean?"

"Where did you hear that word?"

"I overheard a woman in Sabron say something about them to a little girl. She told the girl that if she didn't do her chores, a Bellen would come and eat her."

Delia signed. "Damned idiot, whoever that woman was."

Lilae folded her arms across her chest and held her blanket tightly. She had waited so long to hear this story, and yet, something told her that she was already a part of it all. "That's what you meant, right?"

"Yes. As we speak, they prepare for war in my home. They have made the Underworld into something it was never meant to be. The Underworld was supposed to be a place for the dead to reconnect with their lost loved ones, and go to their last home." Delia looked off.

Lilae couldn't help but forget that Delia was not of this world. Her home had already been taken, and now she hoped to help Lilae keep hers. "I escaped when Wexcyn killed my brothers and sisters. I was aided by the Ancients, so that I could take you before someone else did."

Lilae rested her head against Delia's shoulder again. She scratched at a mosquito bite. "Tell me, Delia. Where do I fit into all of this? Why did you take me?"

Delia stroked Lilae's hair. "Lilae, you are a remarkable young woman. Do you know that?"

Lilae half smiled as she watched the fire. She didn't want Delia to keep anything from her anymore, so she tried to look as if she were brave. "No more stalling, Delia. Go on—tell me. Am I an Ancient or something?" she joked.

Delia didn't say anything. Instead, she pulled back and stared at Lilae. "What did you say?"

Lilae sat up straight. "What? I was joking."

Delia's face was paler than Lilae had ever seen it. She narrowed her eyes at Lilae so that only a small glow replaced her irises. Lilae shuddered. "What is it?"

Delia shook her head. "Lilae, I don't know what possessed you to say that. You are too smart for your own good."

"You're not saying..."

Delia shook her head and waved her hands. "No. No, you're not an Ancient."

Lilae sighed in relief. "That's a relief." Her shoulders slumped. "What then?"

"You were close. You are of the Chosen class—a half god of sorts. With the end of the Great War, the losing Ancients fled, and Wexcyn, the leader, was imprisoned. As a truce, The Barriers were created. However, the truce said that one day another war would be fought... This time for total domination.

But here is the thing, Lilae. It was agreed that each race would produce an heir of the Ancients. You are Telryd's heir."

"How is such a thing possible?"

Delia sat up and leaned a little closer to Lilae, her tone rushing with excitement. "The truce states that the fate of the world would be put in the hands of the people. The Ancients are letting their creations decide who will lead in the Overworld, and there will be no further disputes. They all agreed. It is set in stone. You are the one they call the Flame. You were chosen to lead the humans in this war."

Lilae folded her legs and looked over her shoulder again, feeling as though someone watched her from the dark forest. "You're saying that I will fight Shadow Elves, all to keep Telryd's place secure in the Overworld? Why can't he fight for himself?"

"Lilae, if an Ancient stepped into this world, the balance of power would shift, and the world would not be the same. There's no telling what damage would be done. It must be done by the races."

Lilae squeezed her eyes shut and touched her temples with her fingertips. Her head throbbed. There was just too much to process. "What do I have to do?"

"You will lead the humans against Wexcyn and the forgotten races, and we will hope for the best. For, if you fail, there will be new leadership in the Overworld. Do you understand what that would mean?"

"There would be no more humans."

"Exactly. There would be no more humans, Silver Elves, or Tryans. Shadow Elves will thrive, and Wexcyn will re-create his fallen race." Delia sat back and pulled her cloak tighter. The air grew colder, and the wind picked up speed. "Those of the

Chosen class are all named. You are the Flame, there is also the Storm, the Inquisitor, the Seer, the Steel, and the last is the Cursed. He will be Wexcyn's greatest weapon."

Lilae sighed. "Delia, this is too much." She was having a hard time keeping up a brave front.

"I know that this is a tough fate to accept." Delia leaned back. "I really thought you were ready. I have no choice but to tell you all that I can. Soon, we might not have an opportunity to talk about these things. We must prepare. The Storm is already heading this way. You have to be ready for his arrival. He will be the closest to you, for Pyrii and Telryd are like brothers. Tryans have always been great friends to the humans. As for the other Chosen, they have been ready for years now. We all have been waiting for you."

Lilae stared at the fire. The flames were dying down. She had an odd urge to touch them. Somehow, she knew she could do it. She almost reached out but resisted. She sighed and gazed sidelong at Delia.

"But…" She cleared her throat and tried to straighten her back. "What if I don't want to? Will they replace me? If I am too afraid… can I choose my own path?" Delia shot her a look that made her face pale. She immediately felt embarrassed by her question and looked away.

Delia folded her hands on her lap. "Lilae, dear, I know this must be very hard for you. I've studied human emotion for centuries, and while I do not have such feelings, I am empathetic. But my duty is to see the bigger picture. This entire thing is about more than just you. However, you are the one who must do it. We have waited for someone to be born with all of the necessary power. That someone is you. There will be no replacements."

Lilae looked down at her hands. Delia couldn't understand how she was feeling. She wasn't human and never would be. She was a supernatural being in human flesh. Could Delia even love her? It hurt to think that she was just business to Delia.

Delia noticed the look in Lilae's eyes. She put a hand on Lilae's. "You are strong, Lilae. You can do this."

So, there are five others out there just like me. I wonder if they are as miserable with this burning power as I am. Somehow, she couldn't tell Delia that she had been feeling stranger than normal lately, that she could feel the power that Delia was telling her about. It kept her awake at night, begging to be released.

"I'm afraid, Delia." She avoided eye contact with the Elder. She said it calmly, but she could feel the fear rising in her throat, making her almost giddy. "Is that normal?"

"It's the most normal emotion of them all, my dear."

Lilae pulled her blankets closer. "At least that part of me is human enough." She stared up at the stars, listening to the fire crackle.

"Good girl," Delia smiled and kissed her forehead. "You are the best choice the Ancients could have made, and one day, you'll understand why."

Lilae smiled. She felt comforted by Delia's kiss. Such affection was so rare from her.

Delia stood. "Let's return to camp before the others wake up."

Lilae nodded and followed her back through the forest. When they returned, everyone was still asleep. Delia kept the shield up and put her bedroll beside the fire. She leaned her staff against the wall and watched Lilae as she stood staring past the shield into the darkness.

"Get some rest, Lilae. We will be reaching new territory soon enough." Delia moved away from the fire and pulled her blanket over her. "Soon," Delia said, and smiled at her warmly, "you'll see a real spring."

Lilae nodded absently and grabbed her pack.

"Good night, Delia." She sat down and looked into the fire. She had so much information to process. Lilae always knew she was different, but now that she finally started to realize what was brewing inside, it frightened her.

She looked over her shoulder and into the woods. The quiet all around her made the hairs on her arm stand on end just thinking that Wexcyn was there, watching her. She lay on her bedroll and folded her arms across her chest as her mind drifted, wondering if the other chosen ones were as afraid as she was.

ABOUT THE AUTHOR

K.N. Lee is a New York Times and USA Today bestselling author who resides in Charlotte, North Carolina. When she is not writing twisted tales, fantasy novels, and dark poetry, she does a great deal of traveling and promotes other authors. Wannabe rockstar, foreign language enthusiast, and anime geek, K.N. Lee also enjoys helping others reach their writing and publishing goals. She is a winner of the Elevate Lifestyle Top 30 Under 30 "Future Leaders of Charlotte" award for her success as a writer, business owner, and for community service.

Author, K.N. Lee loves hearing from fans and readers.

CONNECT WITH HER!

Facebook: www.facebook.com/KNycoleLee

Newsletter ow.ly/H28Nb

Twitter: www.twitter.com/knycole_Lee

Website: www.knlee.com

MORE GREAT READS BY, K.N. LEE

Netherworld (Urban Paranormal Fantasy) Demons, ghouls, vampires, and Syths? The Netherworld Division are an organization of angels and humans who are there to keep the escaped creatures from The Netherworld in check in this action-packed paranormal thriller.

Introducing Koa Ryeo-won, a half-blood vampire with an enchanted sword, a membership to the most elite vampire castle in Europe, and the gift of flight. If only she could manage to reclaim the lost memories of her years in The Netherworld, she might finally be able to move forward.

The Scarlett Legacy (Young Adult Fantasy) Wizards. Shifters. Sexy mobsters with magic.

Evie Scarlett is a young wizard who yearns from an escape from her family's bitter rivalry with another crime family. But this time she may be the only one who can save them.

Goddess of War (Young Adult Fantasy) Unsuspecting humans. Fallen gods in disguise. A battle for the entire universe.

After escaping the Vault, a prison for gods, twin siblings Preeti and Vineet make a desperate journey to the human world where they must impersonate the race they are meant to rule and protect.

Silenced (New Adult – Paranormal Romance) Silence kept her alive. Magic will set her free.

Willa Avery created the serum that changed the world as humans, witches, and vampires knew it.

Academia of the Beast (New Adult- Paranormal Romance)

K.N. Lee presents a dark twist on a classic fairy-tale that asks the question: what if the beauty was the mortal enemy of the beast?

Raised in fear of her power.

Sold and betrayed by her lover.

Allyn escaped the hunters once before. As a witch, she risks capture every day.

Liquid Lust (New Adult Romance) Sohana needed a fresh start.

Arthur--a British billionaire has an enticing offer.

Neither expected their arrangement to spark something more.

Spell Slinger (Fantasy Romance/Steampunk)

Lady by day.

Evil fighting vigilante by night.

Yara Ortuso always knew she'd follow in her father's footsteps as a Spell Slinger--until her mother sold her off as a concubine to a lord, after a forbidden romance

Discover more books and learn more about K.N. Lee on knlee.com.

Also by K.N. Lee

The Chronicles of Koa Series:
Netherworld
Dark Prophet
Lyrinian Blade

The Eura Chronicles:
Rise of the Flame
Night of the Storm
Dawn of the Forgotten (Coming Soon)
The Darkest Day (Coming Soon)

The Grand Elite Caster Trilogy:
Silenced
Summoned (Coming Soon)
Awakened (Coming Soon)

The Fallen Gods Trilogy:
Goddess of War
Goddess of Ruin (Coming Soon)
Love & Law (Coming Soon)

Standalone Novellas:
The Scarlett Legacy
Liquid Lust
Spell Slinger

Made in the USA
Columbia, SC
03 October 2017